I0627734

Loving Lydia

Loving Lydia

A Pride and Prejudice Variation

LEENIE BROWN

LEENIE B BOOKS
HALIFAX

Contents

Dear Reader,

Once upon a time...well, actually, a couple of years ago, I began a weekly writing exercise on my blog (leeniebrown.com) and called it Thursday's Three Hundred. What was supposed to be just a few minutes of practice – just three hundred words a week – quickly took on a life of its own and became something much grander.

To date, those writing exercises have produced one short story (*Hope at Dawn*), a four-book series (*Willow Hall Romance*), a stand-alone novella (*With the Colonel's Help*), the first and second books in this series (*Confounding Caroline* and *Delighting Mrs. Bennet*) and now, this novel that you hold in your hand.

While some things about how I create these stories have evolved since that first writing exercise, the tradition of posting a portion of a work in progress continues each Thursday. In fact, there is a new story posting there now.

Chapter 1

"Are you certain you will be well?" Fitzwilliam Darcy asked as he leaned against the doorframe while his sister, Georgiana, worked on getting settled into her room at Netherfield, and Dash sniffed his way around the perimeter of the room.

Why he had allowed two young ladies to talk him into bringing that dog, he was not certain. It was likely his inability to say no to two sets of begging eyes. He shook his head. It was perhaps not his sister about whom he needed to worry. It was himself. He was becoming soft – dreadfully soft.

He reached down and scratched Dash's ear when he came to sniff Darcy's boots for the third time.

"I am certain I will survive if I have to see him. I am not without friends or you." Georgiana turned and looked at him while still holding her jewelry box. She always saw to the arranging of her dressing table. "I am not so foolish as I once was. I do not trust him, and I know for a fact that Miss Lydia and Miss Kitty no longer like him either. You have very little to fear."

"I will worry nonetheless."

She smiled. "Of course, you will. You are most proficient at worrying about me."

It was true. Darcy did excel at worrying about many things – his sister had been at the top of that list, followed very closely by his cousin Colonel Richard Fitzwilliam. However, Georgiana would now find that top position a trifle more crowded. For there was now Elizabeth and her sisters – most especially Miss Lydia – about whom to worry.

"There." Georgiana stepped back and admired her table. "Everything is just as it should be." She glanced around the room. "Where is Dash?"

Darcy sighed and pushed off the doorframe. "He must have escaped."

"Which is not hard to do when the door is standing open," Georgiana teased.

"You have grown a tad impertinent over the past few weeks." Darcy's scold was gentle.

"And your smile says you are not truly displeased," Georgiana said as she crossed the room to where he stood and accepted his proffered arm.

"I cannot say that I am," Darcy agreed. "That is I am not as long as your impertinence keeps its place."

"Which is not in public," Georgiana replied.

"Precisely."

"What is the cause of that sigh?"

Darcy grimaced. He had not meant to sigh, but thoughts of impertinence and worry naturally turned his mind to Lydia Bennet. "I was remembering my promise to Richard."

"What promise is that?"

"I am not certain I should say."

"Is it that dreadful?" Her tone was teasingly horrified.

He chuckled. "That depends on how you receive the information. I know Miss Lydia is your friend."

"Please? I know Richard loves her and that he has asked for permission to write to her while he is away."

Darcy nodded. That was all true. But how did he explain the rest? "This might be said badly," he cautioned. "Richard asked me to help Miss Lydia improve."

"Improve what?" His sister's brow was furrowed as she attempted to understand his meaning.

"Her behaviour in public is not precisely how it should be." Though the comment was critical, Darcy kept his tone gentle. He was not attempting to disparage Miss Lydia. He could not in good conscience denigrate any of Elizabeth's sisters, most especially not the one who held his cousin's heart. However, the truth could not be overlooked either.

"Oh! I had not considered it, but I do see what you mean. She does speak more freely than I was taught to do."

"And her choices of topics are not always the best – such as asking you if you had a beau upon your first meeting."

Georgiana nodded her head thoughtfully. "I understand. It could put her in a place to be ridiculed and hurt. Richard would never wish for that."

"Indeed, he would not." It impressed Darcy how Georgiana had so succinctly stated what the jumbled mess of thoughts in his mind seemed unable to tell him clearly. "I could not have said it better. That is it precisely."

Georgiana patted his arm. "Then we have nothing to fear. I shall behave properly as I usually do, and Mrs. Annesley can assist us. I shall have her spend some time teaching me things that I already know, but that Miss Lydia and Miss Kitty might not know."

It seemed as if it was a plan which might work, but... "I do not wish to tax Mrs. Annesley too much."

"I will ask her, and if she so much as hesitates in replying, I will think of another plan that shall be just as good."

Darcy grimaced as he heard a crash in the drawing room. "I think we have found Dash."

As suspected, Dash was in the drawing room next to a vase which lay in pieces on the floor.

"It was not him," Darcy's friend, Charles Bingley, said in response to Darcy's growled *Dash.*

"Did I tell you I acquired a kitten for Miss Bennet?" Bingley added.

Darcy blinked and looked at Bingley. "You did what?"

"Before I left town, Miss Bennet was telling me about a cat she once had which had run away during a storm. She seemed to miss it a great deal, so when I arrived, I sought out Sir William and inquired if he knew where I might find a grey tabby cat. As luck would have it, he knew precisely where I might find one." Bingley lifted the drapes out of the way and scooped up a kitten. "This is Oliver. He has yet to learn not to push vases off tables."

Bingley crossed the room to where Dash sat. "Dash, this is Oliver," he said, crouching down.

When Dash sniffed the creature, Oliver meowed and attempted to climb Bingley's arm.

"He is a friend," Bingley scolded.

"You are talking to a cat as if he can understand you," Darcy said flatly.

"Who is to say he cannot," Bingley returned. "I think it would be best if they become friends."

"This is what you were doing for two days before we arrived? Acquiring a kitten?"

Bingley released Oliver who looked at Dash for only a moment before returning to his hiding spot behind the drapery.

"No, no, I was also making certain all was ready for your arrival." Bingley blew out a breath. "And that of my sister. She arrives tomorrow."

"Sir Matthew will be joining her, will he not?" Georgiana asked.

"Thankfully, yes." Bingley's eyes shifted from

Darcy and Georgiana to the window. "No, Oliver. He is a friend."

"Perhaps Dash should be made comfortable in your room," Darcy suggested to his sister.

Dash had gone to attempt to make friends with Oliver, but Oliver was none too complacent about the whole idea and had decided it would be best to climb to safety.

"This might not have been my best idea," Bingley said with a laugh as he tried to extricate Oliver's sharp claws from the fabric of the drapes.

"I am certain Miss Bennet will appreciate the gesture," Darcy assured him. He sighed. "I brought Dash for Georgiana and Miss Lydia." He shrugged when Bingley looked at him. "I found it impossible to not grant their request."

Bingley laughed. "What has become of us?"

Darcy took a seat next to his friend. "We have found love, my friend, and it seems love addles one's brain."

Bingley shook his head. "No, our brains are not addled. We are just willing to do that which we might not otherwise do to see those we love happy."

"You do surprise me with your occasional astuteness," Darcy teased.

"I am impressive, am I not? If only Richard were here to tell me I was not."

Darcy sighed and nodded. How he wished the same! And he did not wish it just because then Richard could worry about Miss Lydia. Nor did he wish it just to have Richard here to tease and taunt. He wished it because then he knew his cousin would be safe and not in harm's way.

"I suspect I will receive some news of him soon, letting me know he has arrived in Manchester. That frame-breaking bill will surely stir up more strife than it is intended to squelch."

"I cannot say I blame the frame-breakers for their anger. I have witnessed some very grim living arrangements. However, as the son of a manufacturer, I cannot condone their actions either."

Both men sat in silence for some time. Darcy tapped his fingers on the arm of his chair, while Bingley ran his hand along Oliver's back, who was sleeping on his lap.

"I am sure he will be well," Bingley said at last, putting into words what both men were contemplating.

"He has survived worse," Darcy agreed. While he disliked the idea of Richard being in harm's way at all, he knew it was part and parcel of being a colonel in His Majesty's Forces. And, to Darcy's mind, it was better for Richard to be here, in England, rather than in France, where he had been in the past. While there might be some skirmishes in the North, they were unlikely to be as deadly as a battle on the continent.

Bingley rose from his chair with Oliver tucked in the crook of his arm. "I had planned on calling at Longbourn today for a few minutes. Will you and Georgiana be joining me?"

Darcy smiled. "Without a doubt." It had been nearly a full day since he had seen Elizabeth, and there was only so long a gentleman could go without seeing the lady he loved when he was used to having her under his roof where he could see her at all hours of the day. He was not entirely sure how he was going to survive three miles of separation.

His eyes narrowed as he looked at Bingley. "Do you suppose Oliver could cause some calamity that would require both Miss Bennet and Miss Elizabeth to take up residence here?"

Bingley chuckled. "I do not think I am that clever."

Darcy sighed. "Neither am I, unfortunately, so I suppose, I will have to do as regular gentlemen do and call on her at home."

Chapter 2

"Come in. Come in." Mrs. Bennet urged her callers to enter the sitting room at Longbourn. "It is so good to see you. I was only just telling Mrs. Long – she was here just before you arrived – how anxious I was to know if everyone was settling into Netherfield well and if you found it as pleasing upon your return as you did when you first arrived last autumn." She looked at them expectantly.

"It was just as I left it," Bingley answered. "Although there was no snow in November, so that is new."

"Is it not beautiful?" Kitty asked. "I love how the snow makes everything so bright."

"Beautiful but cold," Bingley answered. "Not that I am unfamiliar with the chill of winter having grown up in the North. I just do not prefer it."

"And you, Miss Darcy," Mrs. Bennet continued. "How do you find Netherfield?"

"It is lovely," Georgiana replied.

"Do you like the snow?"

Georgiana shrugged. "I suppose I do."

"Very good." Mrs. Bennet settled into her chair, seemingly pleased with all she had heard. Then, with a small gasp, she sat forward. "Forgive me. I forgot to inquire about you, Mr. Darcy. You were so quiet slipping in to sit by my Lizzy. I can assure you that Mrs. Long was astounded to hear of my good fortune in having two daughters so well-matched with a third in a very hopeful position. It is indeed a great blessing, I told her. However, one must not be too startled that my daughters have done so well. Just look at them. There is not a plain one amongst the lot. They are all quite beautiful. Well, then, she had a comment or two to say about Mary's disapproving looks, but I assured her that if Lizzy's odd love of books and learning could capture the affections of a man such as yourself, Mr. Darcy, that I was certain that Mary's stern looks and reprimands might be admired by some-one...someday." Her brow furrowed, and she looked past Darcy. "However, it would be lovely if she were to not scold so often. There is a danger of being thought a harridan – which, of course, she is not. None of my girls are." She sighed. The furrow between her eyes deepened for a moment and then faded as she relaxed into her chair, once again pleased with all that had been said.

Darcy pondered her sigh and look of contemplation for a moment. He imagined that it was likely due to her concern about seeing Miss Mary happily married someday. He would have to give some thought to how he might assist her in seeing it done, for seeing one's daughters well-matched must be a great worry for any mother with several daughters.

"I must say that I found Netherfield much improved," he admitted. "The neighbourhood seemed more welcoming and the ladies of the area – one in particular – more beautiful than I remember."

Mrs. Bennet tittered and waved away his words with an "I should think so."

"How is Mr. Bennet?" Darcy asked.

"Papa was delighted to be returned to his book room this morning," Jane said. "However, he has returned to his bed to rest his leg just as the doctor said he should."

"Too much activity too quickly is never a good thing for one who is recovering from an injury." Mrs. Bennet's tone and look were serious. "However," she said, brightening, "he has improved so much since that first day I saw him at Darcy House. Such prodigious good care you gave him, Mr. Darcy."

"It was not I who saw to his care."

"It was your house and your physician."

Had Richard been there, Darcy knew he would have chuckled at the look of displeasure Mrs. Bennet wore at Darcy's audacity to argue with her compliment.

"It was also my dog which caused the injury." Darcy bit back a smile at seeing Mrs. Bennet's eyes narrow for a moment at his continued disagreement. "However, I was happy to be of service to both Mr. Bennet and the rest of your family. I would not be lying if I said Darcy House was exceptionally lonely yesterday after your departure. I am delighted to be here amongst you all."

That earned him a delighted smile.

"I can barely believe it." Elizabeth's tone was

teasing. "I thought that you preferred solitude to company."

Darcy chuckled. "I did until I learned just how comforting company of the right sort can be." He lifted her hand to his lips, which he knew was far too forward but which he also knew would continue to delight Mrs. Bennet, and strangely, very strangely, indeed, he had come to find great pleasure in pleasing the Bennet matriarch.

"Have you had a letter?" Lydia asked.

Darcy shook his head. "Not yet. I am certain there will be one soon, however."

"You will tell me as soon as you can if you receive one?"

Darcy nodded. "And you will do the same?"

"Without question! Why I could no better keep such a thing to myself as Lizzy could refrain from reading for a full day. It is just not in my nature to keep such a pleasurable thing to myself. It must be shared with someone, and you do seem like the best person with whom to share such a thing." Her brow furrowed, and she drew the right corner of her lower lip between her teeth.

"I am certain it will contain many interesting

stories when it arrives," Darcy assured her. "Richard is a most excellent storyteller."

Her features relaxed, and she gave him a small thankful smile before turning to Kitty and Georgiana.

"As you know, she has not been quite herself," Elizabeth whispered.

"Or herself has been permanently altered by concerns beyond herself," Darcy whispered in reply. "Georgiana is altered after her first encounter with imagined love – not that either Richard or Lydia's care for the other is imagined," he clarified when Elizabeth's left eyebrow rose. "I am just saying that love, whether real or imagined, has an altering effect on a person."

"Does it?"

Darcy tipped his head and silently looked at her lovely face for a moment until she began to squirm. "I am certain it was love which caused me to enter into that scheme to see Caroline wed to Sir Matthew, and I know that it was love which caused me to expose myself to your family, which in turn has forever changed how I view the silence of my home." He squeezed the hand of hers that he still held. "They are very good changes. Even the changes in Georgiana are not all bad. She has gained wisdom, though I wish she had not gained it in such a fashion."

So much had changed inside of him since he had allowed love to rule over duty in his heart. He would not wish to return to his former self. It was as if loving Elizabeth had awakened something – had caused that something to blossom and flourish – a something that had lain dormant for some time.

"Are you unaltered by love?" he asked.

Elizabeth shook her head. "I see things so differently now. Do you truly think that is what is happening for my sister?"

"I can only suppose." Darcy rose as Lady Lucas, and her youngest daughter entered the room. He bowed and did all that was proper as he and his sister were introduced.

"So my husband was not wrong!" Lady Lucas cried. "Oh, he will be quite pleased to hear it. He will insist we have a soiree with dancing. Perhaps this time, Miss Elizabeth would be more willing to participate in the dancing." Her eyebrows flicked up as she said it. "Does Charlotte know of your betrothal?" She looked at Mrs. Bennet without waiting for Elizabeth's reply. "I am sending a letter tomorrow. I do it twice a month, you know. It is dreadful and yet not so very much to have one's daughter so far removed, although she is not so far away as some will be." She paused only long enough to take a quick breath. "Will you be remaining at Netherfield, Mr. Bingley?"

Darcy looked at the hand Elizabeth had placed on his arm before his eyes lifted to her face. "I am well," he whispered. "It just might take a little longer to get used to all the neighbours than I had hoped."

"Colonel Fitzwilliam is in Manchester."

Darcy pulled his eyes away from Elizabeth upon hearing his cousins spoken of and looked toward the group of younger ladies seated across from him just as Lydia sighed and covered her heart with her hand in a rather dramatic fashion.

"You should see him in his regimentals. He is quite handsome in a regular suit of clothing but in his regimentals?" Lydia sighed dramatically once again. "Oh, you simply must see the ribbon I purchased when in town, Maria. You do remember how you were always telling me that I should get a red ribbon to go with my sprigged muslin, do you not?"

"Indeed, a red ribbon was just what it needed," Maria agreed.

"You were not wrong." Lydia grasped Maria's hand. "Well! Let me tell you. It was quite the melee, for Mama thought one would suit, and I thought it should be another. Miss Darcy was certain I was right while Kitty thought Mama was. Do you know how we settled it?"

"No, how?" Maria leaned forward eagerly.

"We asked the colonel." Lydia wore a very pleased expression as she lifted her chin. "And he, of course, after a bit of consideration, chose mine."

"He did not!" Maria cried.

Darcy sighed. He did not find the flutterings of young ladies to be particularly enjoyable. Indeed, he found them to be somewhat tedious.

"Are you still certain you can tolerate all of this?" Elizabeth whispered.

"Honestly?"

She nodded when he looked in her direction.

"It will not be easy," Darcy admitted. "However, I do think the prize is worth the discomfort."

Chapter 3

"Lady Lucas was wrong." Bingley dropped a missive next to Darcy's cup of tea the following morning. "This came while we were out riding."

Darcy read the invitation to a soiree at Lucas Lodge. "She did not waste any time, did she?"

Bingley chuckled. "Indeed, she did not. You will accept. Will you not?"

"Of course. I must." Darcy intended to show himself as a changed individual to the community, and, to do so, he must take part in activities where he would be amongst the people of Meryton. He had reparations to make, civilities to bestow – whether they were easily done or not.

"Caroline will likely be less than pleased to accept, but she is named on the invitation," Bingley said.

"This is the first time she will be back under your

roof since she attempted to both separate you from Miss Bennet and force you into marrying another. It could be a trying time for all." Darcy breathed in the steam from his tea before taking a careful sip. He should likely let it cool longer rather than risking a burnt tongue, but the fragrance was so much more welcoming when it rose with the steam.

Across from Darcy, Bingley sighed and sank into his chair. "I will admit to being somewhat nervous to have her here, but she will be with Sir Matthew. And he seems to have had a settling effect on her, according to Hurst."

"And she arrives this afternoon?"

"Yes. But first, I hear you are off to do some shopping."

Darcy smiled over his teacup. "I tell you, Bingley, I am becoming soft."

Bingley laughed. "Not this time. I know your true reason. The militia is still in town; the winter is not yet over."

It was true. The militia's presence was bothersome to Darcy.

Georgiana and the youngest Miss Bennets wished to visit the shops in Meryton. Kitty, in particular, was eager to show her new friend what could be purchased so close to Longbourn. Georgiana had insisted that they only needed Mrs. Annesley to accompany them, but Darcy was more insistent that he join her for at least this first outing.

Wickham might be returned to his unit, and even though Darcy and Richard had pummelled him – and maybe even because of it – the gentleman might not remain quiet about what he knew concerning Georgiana, Lydia, or Elizabeth. It was better in Darcy's mind for Wickham to be met by himself and not just his sister and her friends.

"I am coming with you," Bingley added.

Darcy's eyebrows rose as he swallowed the sip of tea he had taken.

"Miss Bennet is going to attend her sisters," Bingley explained.

"So is Miss Elizabeth."

It was Elizabeth's presence that made the thought of entering shops to look at lace, gloves, hats, and the like more than bearable. Not only would Darcy be able to stroll the high street with her on his arm, but he would also get the chance to see what sorts of things caught her eye when she entered the shops. He had a wedding that was not too far in the future, and he wished to present her with something he knew she would enjoy and perhaps even cherish.

He cradled his cup of tea. His mother had a box for her broaches that had been given to her by his father. The top had been carved with bluebells, her favourite flower, and the interior was lined in purple silk because it was her favourite colour.

It was details such as these that Darcy knew he still needed to learn about Elizabeth. Of course, if observation failed, he could always inquire about such details from one of her sisters. Or, he supposed, he could just ask Elizabeth, though he did wish for his gift to be a surprise.

"I see there was more unrest." Bingley passed the newspaper to Darcy, who blew out a breath.

"I would almost rather not know," he said.

"It was in Yorkshire, not Manchester," Bingley added as Darcy began to read the account in the paper.

Sadly, the reports of damages done to property and of shots fired at protestors were becoming as commonplace as the reports of unrest on the continent.

"It is not so very far from him." Darcy sighed and

wondered if Lydia ever read the paper. He hoped she did not.

A more startling thought caused him to suck in a breath just as he was taking a sip of tea. This, in turn, set off a fit of coughing and sputtering. "I am well," he assured Bingley as soon as he was able before coughing for a bit longer.

"Was there something startling in the paper?"

Darcy shook his head and took a proper sip of tea instead of attempting to inhale the liquid. "No, I was just wondering if Mrs. Bennet ever reads the paper." He pulled back from the table in surprise when Oliver landed near his plate.

"You are not allowed on the table," Bingley scolded, scooping up the kitten before it could scamper away. "I doubt she does. However, I would not be surprised if both Miss Elizabeth and Miss Mary read it."

Darcy groaned. "And Miss Mary might find it her duty to inform her mother and sisters of events. You know that kitten might find it less enjoyable to attack the tables and curtains if you did not pluck him from where he should not be and reward him by tucking him in for a pet."

Oliver was happily curled in Bingley's lap and purring.

"You scold almost as well as Miss Mary," Bingley replied with a laugh before reaching for his tea.

Either Bingley's laugh or his movement stirred the purring cat from his repose. Startled, the animal leapt up and, in so doing, caused Bingley's tea to spill. The kitten escaped the sloshing liquid. However, Bingley's breeches did not. With a muttered curse, Bingley rose. "It seems I am going to change for our outing now rather than later."

Before leaving the room, Bingley scowled at Oliver, who was hiding behind the leg of the sideboard. "You had best hope Miss Bennet likes you, or you might find yourself in the stables. Tea on my trousers. Of all the things."

Darcy could hear him continuing to mutter as he exited the room. No sooner was Bingley out of sight than Oliver slinked out from hiding and headed in Darcy's direction.

"You will have no luck with me." Darcy swallowed the last of his tea, rose, and left the room with Oliver trailing behind. "Oh, very well." Darcy stooped and gave the kitten's head a scratch, earning himself a contented purr. "Now, stay here."

Unfortunately, Oliver was as well behaved as a certain pup, and Darcy had to be quick to enter his room without company. Between animals and young ladies, Darcy was certain this sojourn at Netherfield was going to be excessively trying.

He sighed.

"And Caroline arrives this afternoon, and Wickham might be in Meryton." He shook his head at his reflection in the mirror and then rang for his man.

~*~*~

An hour later, after Darcy had changed from his riding clothes and spent a leisurely half hour reading in his room, which was blessedly free from distractions, he, Bingley, Georgiana, and Mrs. Annesley arrived at Longbourn. From here, Georgiana and Mrs. Annesley would travel with the younger Bennets while the oldest Bennets would ride with Darcy and Bingley.

"Good morning, Fitzwilliam," Elizabeth whispered as she took his hand so that he could help her into the carriage.

"Good morning, Elizabeth," he replied, lifting her hand to kiss it. "Not there," he said when she sat down on the bench next to Jane.

"Then where?"

"With me." He turned to Bingley. "You do not mind giving up your place next to me to Miss Elizabeth, do you?"

Chuckling, Bingley shook his head and entered the carriage.

"Oh, Mr. Darcy!" Lydia cried, poking her head out of the door to the Bennet's carriage. "I have a letter. I nearly forgot. I do not know how I could have. It is likely the excitement of everything." She waved an envelope at him.

"Do you wish me to read it?" he asked. "Is it not private?"

Her eyes lowered, and she blushed.

"Parts of it may be," she replied coyly. "However, if you do not read the last paragraph... He said to give you and Miss Darcy his love in that part." She still held out the letter.

"Are you certain?" Darcy questioned once more. There was no way he was going to intrude on Miss Lydia's or Richard's privacy.

"Just the beginning," Lydia said with a nod of her head.

"I promise not to read the last paragraph, and I thank you for your trust." Darcy took the missive from her. "I will have it read before we enter the first store, and then you may safely hide it away."

Lydia thanked him and pulled her head back into the carriage.

He greatly felt the honour of being allowed the privilege of reading a letter not addressed to him. And so, once he was settled into his carriage again, he immediately set about reading what Richard had written, taking care not to allow his eyes to even skim the final paragraph.

"What does he have to say?" Bingley asked.

"He has settled into his accommodations – he is staying at an inn, it seems. The room is not large, and the innkeeper's wife is not small." He chuckled at Richard's description of the jovial couple that ran the inn. It seemed his cousin may have found a friendly place to rest his head at night. As long as...

"Does he say what the innkeeper thinks of the unrest." Bingley put Darcy's concern into words.

Darcy shook his head. "There is little talk about any unrest in this letter, and what is here is couched in such a fashion that it does not appear to be of any significance. However, I suspect there will be more about that when he writes to me. Hopefully, he will include a section of the letter that I will be able to give to Miss Lydia to read. I have no great desire to see her unnecessarily unsettled."

"The paper had an account in it," Jane said. "But Lydia does not read that portion of the paper. In fact, I am not certain she knows what is in a paper other than what the society pages say. And Papa would not allow her to read anything else."

"But he allows you?"

Jane nodded. "And Lizzy and Mary. However, we have all been warned most sternly that we are not to speak of it to either Mama or our sisters."

"Papa does not wish to deal with the fit of nerves it would produce," Elizabeth added.

Darcy pulled in a deep breath and released it. "I had worried Miss Lydia might hear about things. I am glad she will not."

"Why Mr. Darcy," Elizabeth teased, "might you actually care for my youngest sister?" Her eyes were not laughing as her tone might indicate they should be.

"How can I not?" he replied with a soft smile for her. "We are to be related."

Elizabeth wrapped her arm around his and squeezed it tightly.

For her, he could weather a great many annoyances – excessively talkative neighbours, the high spirits of young ladies, and even the affection demanded by animals. However, at present, those annoyances held only a small space in his mind for he had spied a group of redcoats in front of some establishment as the carriages entered the high street in Meryton.

Chapter 4

"Did you see Mr. Wickham in that group?" Jane whispered across the carriage to Elizabeth as the door was opened and the steps were put in place.

"I did not, but then I could not see every face. Did you?" Elizabeth did not need to hear Darcy's response for one look at the set of his jaw was all the only reply she needed. "He is here?"

Darcy nodded.

"Perhaps he will be wise and keep his distance," Bingley said hopefully as he climbed out of the carriage. "But even if he proves to be the fool we know him to be, Darcy and I will see to him."

"You will not cause a scene in the high street, will you?" Jane asked in surprise. Elizabeth could well imagine the anxiety such a thing must cause for Jane for the thought of it caused her own heart to beat a little faster.

"Not unless it is necessary," Darcy answered.

Bingley nodded. "Creating a scene is far better than allowing anything to happen to those we love."

"Indeed!" Darcy agreed with enthusiasm.

"But the talk from such a thing..." Jane cautioned as she stepped down from the carriage. She straightened her pelisse and touched her hat to see that it was properly secure as a small smile played at her lips. "I could always trip him. Who might we match him with, Lizzy?"

"I cannot think of a single young lady who deserves such a husband!" Elizabeth cried. This teasing and taunting side of Jane had always lain hidden behind the closed doors of Longbourn, so it was pleasantly shocking to have it so displayed.

"Oh, I am not entirely certain of that," Jane retorted as she placed her hand on Bingley's arm. "Mrs. Salter might have a relation who favours her."

Darcy's laugh in response to the suggestion caused Elizabeth's own laugh to die on her lips.

"I had forgotten that you have both delved into your devious sides," Elizabeth said, looking up at the formerly dour Mr. Darcy.

"If Darcy continues to be so animated," Bingley inserted before either Jane or Darcy could defend themselves to Elizabeth, "we are certain to draw a crowd to gaze on the strange spectacle of the jovial gentleman from Derbyshire."

Darcy's left brow rose, and he peered down his nose at his friend. It might have been a convincing look of hauteur had his lips not twitched in an attempt to contain a smile that would not be entirely suppressed. "You are correct, of course. I am not the man I was when I was last here." He sighed and glanced up and down the street.

"I think it was just there," he pointed to a shop opposite them and a short distance away, "where we first met Mr. Wickham in Meryton. I wanted to run him through then, which is not so different from how I feel now. However, then, I was more reserved. I had my sister's reputation to consider, and I knew few and cared for even fewer members of this village and its environs. Now, there is not only my sister to defend but also the lady I love and her sisters to consider. I fear I might not be able to conjure the appropriate amount of reserve to resist treating him now as I wished to then."

Elizabeth seemed doomed to always be provoked

to smile a silly little grin every time Darcy spoke so openly of his care for her. At the moment, he seemed unaware of any shopkeepers or shoppers who might be within hearing distance.

"Why should you need reserve?" Lydia asked. She and the others had just joined them.

"Your letter, Miss Lydia." Darcy withdrew the folded missive from his pocket and handed it to her. "Again, I thank you for the privilege of reading the beginning of it."

"You did not read the last paragraph?" she asked as she slipped the letter into her reticule.

"Not a word of it."

Elizabeth watched the exchange with interest. Lydia was so different and yet the same since her trip to London. There was a softening of her boisterous edges as the small thank you to Darcy demonstrated so well.

"We should like to view some muslin." Lydia looked to her companions, Kitty and Georgiana, who both nodded. "And Miss Darcy would like to see what sorts of music might be acquired here in Meryton." She glanced at Mrs. Annesley. "If that would be acceptable to you."

"I think those are fine items for which to look," Darcy replied.

Elizabeth was quite impressed by her sister's demeanor until they were just about to go in search of their first store.

"You have still not told me why you need to gather your reserve?" She fluttered her lashes at Darcy and smiled.

"Ah... well..." Darcy began haltingly, "that has to do with the fact that a particular member of the militia is returned from town to Meryton."

Lydia gasped, and her hand flew to her mouth. "I do hope he is returned!"

"I beg your pardon?" Elizabeth's reply was quick. Why would her sister wish to see Mr. Wickham after the way he had treated them?

"Well, I should like to see the bruises the colonel and Mr. Darcy gave him. I am certain it would be very romantic to witness the defense of one's honour. And should Mr. Darcy not be able to find his reserve, we might get to witness not just the traces of a former altercation."

"I am certain I would not like to see him or his bruises," Georgiana said.

Elizabeth did not miss the small look of apology that passed from Georgiana to her brother.

"It is not that I think myself unable to see him," Georgiana added quickly. "I just do not think it proper to find such injuries to be pleasing."

"No, not at all," Mrs. Annesley encouraged. "Nor should one wish to be reminded of one's folly."

The comment was said very softly, and the accompanying look was just as gentle.

Lydia gasped, a look of mortification spreading across her face for a moment before being tucked away. "I had not thought of it as such. You are very right, Mrs. Annesley. I should not like to be reminded of my foolishness."

"Nor do you wish to have it broadcast about," Mrs. Annesley continued in the same calm tone.

"No, no. I am sure I do not," Lydia agreed. "I am certain I do not wish to see him at all. Indeed, I wish he were still in London."

"Richard would be pleased to hear you say so," Darcy added.

That sealed the fate of wishing to see either Mr. Wickham or his bruises.

"He is not even here," Elizabeth whispered when

her younger sisters and Georgiana, accompanied by Mrs. Annesley, had moved ahead of them by a few paces, "and still the colonel is seeing to Lydia's improvement."

"It is remarkable," Jane agreed. "As is Mrs. Annesley," she added.

"Indeed, she is," Darcy agreed. "My sister was certain she and Mrs. Annesley could help me see to Miss Lydia's continued improvement as I promised Richard I would do."

This was not news to either Elizabeth or Jane. Darcy had told Elizabeth of his promise to Richard, and Elizabeth had, in turn, shared it with Jane.

Elizabeth pressed her hand more firmly on Darcy's arm at the sound of his soft but heavy sigh.

He turned questioning eyes towards her.

"I, too, wish he were here," she whispered, earning herself a smile of appreciation.

Ahead of them, Lydia was standing in front of a store peering through its many-paned window with Kitty on her one side and Georgiana on her other. Mary stood behind them with Miss Annesley, looking as if she was embarrassed to be seen in front of a shop window.

"Does Miss Mary not enjoy shopping?"

Apparently, Darcy had noticed Mary's unease as well.

"Mary prefers a list of items to be purchased and a rapid walk from merchant to merchant before meandering home while reading, satisfied to know that everything she needs will be delivered shortly," Jane replied.

"Save for the few small treats she might have purchased to eat while she walks," Elizabeth added. "Those she will carry, of course."

"A lady with purpose," Darcy muttered, "is not a bad thing."

"Unless she thinks everyone should conform to her way of thinking," Jane cautioned. "That would be Mary's weakness."

They had nearly reached the shop where their sisters stood when to Elizabeth's dismay, the group of officers they had seen, crossed the street.

"We have only just arrived back at Longbourn," Kitty was saying to Captain Denny as Elizabeth and Darcy joined her. "And we thought to show our friend the high street. Have you seen if there is any new music at the bookseller's?"

"I cannot say I have inquired." Denny shifted and glanced uneasily at Darcy. "At least, I have not since I sent my sister that piece of music last month. You remember the one, do you not?"

"Oh, indeed, I do," Kitty replied, smiling broadly. "It would be lovely if they still had a copy."

"We shall have to make certain to stop there," Elizabeth inserted before extending her greeting to the assembled officers.

Wickham glanced first at her face and then the hand which lay on Darcy's arm. "I understand that you and Miss Bennet have happy news. Allow me to extend my joy." He gave each of them a small bow of his head.

The comment surprised Elizabeth, although not because he knew of her betrothal – for, if Lady Lucas knew, everyone knew. No, she was surprised by the civility with which he greeted them and the fact that he would mention hers or Jane's betrothal at all.

"We only wanted to wish you a happy return to the neighbourhood." Captain Saunders wore a pleasant smile, though his eyes did dart uneasily toward Darcy before returning to the rest of the group. Then, he and his companions bowed and took their leave, wandering down the street toward the inn.

"Well," said Bingley, "that was unexpected."

"His bruises looked impressive," Lydia whispered with a pleased smile for Darcy. "Well done."

"We do not congratulate gentlemen on how well they can bruise another," Mrs. Annesley inserted. "Not even if those bruises are well-deserved." She winked at Lydia. "We have muslins to see."

"Muslins!" Darcy said, sending an amused smile in Bingley's direction.

"Indeed!" Bingley agreed, with a smirk of his own. "I am all anticipation" he teased.

"You poor men," Jane consoled. "What trials you endure!"

"And happily so," Bingley assured her.

"Very happily so," Darcy agreed before lifting Elizabeth's hand and placing a kiss on her knuckles bringing to mind what he had promised her while they were still in London – to endure every possible irritation for her sake.

However, as she stepped into the shop, Elizabeth was not sure if the kiss was because of the gentlemen they had met outside or the cries of delight from three young ladies admiring a selection of muslin.

Chapter 5

To Elizabeth's surprise, Darcy seemed to be settling easily into the neighbourhood. He had greeted a few gentlemen by name when they had been in Meryton three days ago.

"We went shooting together," he had told her.

He had patiently borne all of her mother's happy exclamations each day when a neighbour had come to call while Darcy was also in the sitting room. Then, he had been the one to suggest dancing to Sir William when they were at Lucas Lodge for dinner last evening.

It was remarkable the change he had made, and her heart thrilled to know that he endured it all for her. She was certain there was not another man in all of England who was as wonderful as her Mr. Darcy.

Today, however, he seemed a little out of sorts.

His smile was not as quick as it had been since his arrival, and he was quiet – not that silence was something which was foreign to him. It was just that it felt to her as if the silence was a heavy blanket he had to carry.

"The sun is warm today," Elizabeth said.

Darcy nodded. "It is."

Elizabeth held his arm a little more firmly, moving to walk closer to him as if somehow doing so might help him bear whatever burden he carried. His lips curled up softly as he looked down at her, and the same soft pleasure of his smile shone in his eyes.

"I have had a letter from Richard," he said after a few silent paces down the road.

Jane and Bingley, as well as Caroline and Sir Matthew, were somewhere behind them, while Georgiana and Elizabeth's other sisters were ahead of them. None were close enough to hear a word of Darcy and Elizabeth's conversation.

"I wished to tell you right away, but..." His eyes left hers as he looked toward the group in front of them.

"You did not want Lydia to know?"

He nodded. "I cannot allow her to read it. The

details are," he shook his head, "disturbing, but I have promised to share with her when he writes to me."

"Was there any news which was not disturbing? Perhaps you can share that bit with her?" Elizabeth prodded hopefully.

"There were a few descriptions of his accommodations and a fellow officer or two. It was all written just as Richard would tell me if he were in my study enjoying a glass of port with me."

Elizabeth watched as a small smile played at the corners of Darcy's mouth while, she assumed, he contemplated his cousin.

"He has been injured, but it is not severe. A few stitches above his left eye is all. There was an altercation at a tavern, and a window was broken. He assures me it will only make his appearance more fetching should it scar for it is so small and distinguished looking." He chuckled softly before sobering once again. "But I cannot tell your sister about that or the arrests or people who have died."

"Then do not tell her. Share with her the tales of the officers and tell her that the rest was about things which would surely bore her to tears. She does not wish to read about daily duties, and I am certain the awful bits were, sadly, just part of your cousin's daily duties." Elizabeth squeezed Darcy's arm tightly. How horrible it must be for him to have someone so close to him in harm's way. She had never really contemplated how it must be for some who had loved ones who were on the continent, in a far away colony where there was unrest, or sailing with the navy, let alone here at home locked in a disagreement with fellow countrymen.

"That would not be too great a prevarication, would it?" Darcy asked.

Elizabeth shook her head. "I do not believe it would be. You may tell her about his cut if you wish. I do not think that would cause her too much distress, and she must know that there are dangers."

Darcy expelled a great breath, the weight of resignation and grave duty were in the sound. "I believe you are correct. Shall we catch up to them?"

With Elizabeth's permission, they quickened their pace and were soon able to overtake the young ladies ahead of them. Of course, the fact that their sisters had stopped for Kitty to retie a bootlace did help Darcy and Elizabeth's effort.

"We must turn back soon," Elizabeth said as they reached their sisters.

"But before we do," Darcy began, "I wished to tell you that I have had a letter from my cousin."

"Richard?" Georgiana said eagerly.

Elizabeth looked quickly to Darcy. She had not thought of how his sister might receive this news. Indeed, he had not mentioned it as something which lay heavy on his heart. He had surely thought of his sister, but it was his concern for Lydia that grieved him the most.

Darcy flashed his sister a quick, tight smile and nodded. "I did not bring it to share because it was not all fit for the eyes of young ladies."

"Oh, I should think it is not!" Lydia said, surprising them all. "I would imagine that gentlemen speak to each other in letters as they do when they have their port after dinner."

"What do you mean?" Mary asked.

"Well," said Lydia as the large group started moving forward again, "we ladies are sent away, and I imagine it is so the gentlemen can use vulgar language and speak of indelicate things. Is that not what you do?"

Darcy looked from her inquisitive face to the

others who also peeked at him. "I suppose, sometimes that is the case."

Elizabeth could not help but smile at his uncertain, hesitating tone and the wary expression he wore. It was as if he were uncertain what Lydia might ask him next.

"What did your cousin have to say?" Lydia asked, seemingly satisfied with Darcy's response.

"He told me about the innkeepers just as he told you. Then, he mentioned a fellow – a Captain G – who likes to sing hymns when they go out to patrol but who, after he has had a pint or two, also sings the bawdiest songs Richard has ever heard."

"I can see why that would not be something a young lady should read," muttered Mary.

"Oh, indeed," Darcy agreed. "There was one thing which happened that is not of a pleasant nature to have to report. It seems that during a disagreement between some gentlemen one night at a tavern, a window was broken, and Richard received a cut during the dispute. As a result, he required a few stitches to close the wound, but he assures me that it makes him look very distinguished," Darcy added quickly over the gasps of the four young ladies in their group.

"He is well?" Lydia asked, turning fearful eyes toward Darcy.

Elizabeth wished to gather her into her arms at the sight of her distress. She glanced up at Darcy. His throat moved up and down as he swallowed while he nodded.

"He assures me he is well."

Lydia's shoulders relaxed as she expelled a quiet, relieved breath. "That is very good news then," she said after a moment of silence. "Was there anything else?"

"Nothing I can share," Darcy answered.

"He spoke of fighting?" Lydia asked quietly.

"He did."

"I knew that there could be some," she added. "He told me before he left." She shrugged. "No one wants to lose their livelihood or their lives."

"He told you that?"

Lydia nodded. "I am not a child, Mr. Darcy." She pulled her shoulders straight. "But I thank you for not sharing any of the fightings with me aside from the colonel's injury."

They walked on for some time in silence. Elizabeth was impressed by how Lydia had accepted the news. There were no tears or fits of nerves. Her response had been more reminiscent of how Jane might react rather than how their mother might — which had always been Lydia's normal wont up until now. Lydia was improving. How had Colonel Fitzwilliam known to share such serious matters with her before he left? Elizabeth would have expected him to assure Lydia that he would be well and would return soon. She had not thought he would tell her about the grave nature of his duty. Once again, she was struck by just how very good Colonel Fitzwilliam was for her sister.

Darcy fished in his pocket and withdrew his handkerchief. Then, he touched Lydia's shoulder and gave it to her.

So, there were tears. Elizabeth had not seen them, but Darcy had. She smiled up at him as he wiped at the corners of his own eyes with his hand. Her brow furrowed. Was he thinking of his cousin?

He tipped his head toward Lydia and then touched his heart.

She nodded her understanding before laying her head against his shoulder. He was still thinking of her sister — her youngest, most troublesome sister — and his heart was touched. The thought could only endear him more firmly to her. He truly was the best of men.

Chapter 6

Darcy settled into a comfortable chair in Netherfield's drawing room. Dash lay at his feet, and Oliver stalked them both from the far side of the room. Darcy chuckled over how the curious creature would come within feet of Dash but then scurry away as soon as Dash flinched. The fur above Dash's eyes was moving as he watched Oliver walk to and fro. Eventually, the two might become friends as Bingley predicted, but at present, it appeared as if that was not going to happen any time soon.

"That was not as dreadful as I expected," Caroline Bingley said as she took a seat on a settee. She had attended the soiree at Lucas Lodge after her arrival at Netherfield, but today was the first day she had decided to call on any of the neighbors. "The Bennets seem to improve upon acquaintance, though…" She stopped speaking when Sir Matthew coughed softly.

"There are many in this world who pose some sort of challenge to our sensibilities," Sir Matthew said.

"Oh, indeed, there are!" Caroline agreed. "Mrs. Bennet is an acquired taste."

Sir Matthew shrugged but said nothing.

"She was very welcoming of you, as she should be," Caroline added, placing a hand on her betrothed's arm. "It is not every day that she has a baronet in her home." Caroline turned to Darcy, her smile somewhat smug. "That is what she said."

"It is true," Darcy replied.

Caroline was more accepting of things than he ever remembered her being, but she had still not forgiven him either for rejecting her or for having caused her current betrothed state. Therefore, he would endure her small jabs for as long as she felt it necessary to punish him.

Darcy gave a small shake of his head when Sir Matthew raised an eyebrow in question. The man had met with both Bingley and Darcy within moments of his arrival to discuss how challenging having Caroline under the same roof as them might be. The man was exceptionally good at directing Caroline, but even more surprising was the fact that he did not seem daunted by the task. He had the patience of Job. Nothing seemed to ruffle his calm exterior.

"I am not that important," Sir Matthew said, grasping Caroline's hand which lay on his arm. "I am fortunate to have inherited a title and an estate."

Caroline's head had dipped, and her cheeks grew rosy when he had secured her hand in his.

"I am also fortunate to have fallen for such a lovely lady as yourself." His eyes smiled as much as his lips did.

To Darcy, it looked as if Sir Matthew was truly happy in his current situation.

"I think we will visit Mrs. Philips and Lady Lucas tomorrow."

Dash's head popped up almost as if he were as surprised as Darcy was at hearing Caroline say such a thing, but it was not Caroline's words that had caught Dash's attention. Nor was it Bingley's entrance to the drawing room and his subsequent scooping up of Oliver that had caused Dash to grumble. There was a carriage on the drive.

"Were you expecting visitors?" Sir Matthew asked.

"No. But it could be any one of our neighbours. There are several who have not yet called." Bingley stood expectantly in front of his chair, rather than sitting.

It was not very long before the noise of someone entering drifted up the stairs to the open door of the sitting room.

Dash was the first to move.

Darcy rushed after him, but he was not quick enough to catch him.

"Darcy, what is the meaning of this?" Lady Catherine waved at the dog who was sniffing her shoes. "I nearly fell! It is not a proper way to be greeted. Not at all. Go on with you. Leave me be," she said to Dash, and Dash being the dog that he was, cocked his head to the side, looked up at her, and moved not an inch.

"Dash," Darcy called. The beast removed his eyes from Lady Catherine to consider Darcy for a moment before ignoring him completely.

"It seems he likes you, Aunt Catherine."

"Of all the things!" she huffed. "You know how I

feel about animals in the house. Dogs are for hunting, not decoration."

"Dash is anything but a decoration," Darcy said with a laugh. "And he has yet to learn to hunt. I got him for Georgiana. He makes her happy."

Lady Catherine's right brow rose as her lips pursed and she looked down at Dash. "Well, then, I suppose I must like you. Now stand by and allow me to finish my ascent of these stairs."

Dash plopped down on the step and did not move.

"I must say he obeys well when you speak correctly. I will teach you, Darcy. You are too soft. You always have been, but then, that is what I like about you." She had reached the top of the stairs by the time she had finished her comments. "Come along," she said to Dash, who immediately obeyed. "Anne is in town with her aunt. She is well. The cough never developed into anything of consequence." She looked up and down the hall. "We must talk."

"About what?" Darcy asked before making a move to lead her to the sitting room.

"I have heard tales about a betrothal. That cannot be. You were destined for Anne."

Darcy sighed. "The study is this way." He motioned down the hallway.

"I had a letter – well, no. That is not it precisely. Mrs. Collins had a letter. It contained some very unsettling news."

Apparently, his aunt was not about to wait until they had reached the study before she had her say. Of course, that was not uncommon for his aunt. When she had business to discuss, it was discussed no matter where she might be in the house. Servants did not have ears in her world. At least, they did not if they wished to retain their position in her household.

"I had thought that Mrs. Collins's mother must be mistaken. You could not possibly be betrothed to some young woman since we have been expecting you to offer for Anne for some time now." She entered the study ahead of him and paused speaking long enough to give the room a thorough looking over before sighing with resignation that it would have to do and taking a seat.

"As I was saying, I knew it could not be true, but Mrs. Collins insisted it was. Well, I knew if anyone knew the truth it would be my brother, so we – Anne and I – went to London. You were not home, which caused me no little amount of trepidation, and then, well..." She shook her head and looked most dissatisfied. "My brother informed me that the rumors I had heard were not rumors at all."

"They are not. I am betrothed." Darcy unbuttoned his jacket and reclined in his chair.

"My brother will not support me, but I had to come place my case, as well as that of your very disheartened cousin, before you. How could you play her false?"

Darcy blinked. "Play Anne false?"

Lady Catherine nodded. "She has just finished sewing a cap for when she marries. This news came as quite a blow."

Darcy doubted that very much. Anne had no desire to be Mrs. Darcy. Of that, Darcy was rather certain.

"I do apologize for your disappointment, but it is not I who has played my cousin false, madame. I believe that grievous sin falls to you."

"To me? Of all the... I dare say it does not!"

"You are the only one who has ever spoken to her about marrying me. I know for a fact that I have never mentioned it. I have done nothing to engage her affections. I have been very careful to be as circumspect as can be around my cousin."

Lady Catherine scowled. "You were kind to her."

"As I should be. We are relations." His words only deepened his aunt's scowl. "Nothing you say will move me." It was best to just end this argument before it began. "I am marrying Elizabeth Bennet."

"What is she compared to you?" Lady Catherine grumbled, stirring Darcy's ire.

"She is my life, my heart, my everything, and I will not abide one ill word to be spoken against her. If you wish to retain your relationship with me, you will measure your words carefully."

"Love," she muttered. "Young people these days think love is of utmost importance. Foolish notions. Marriage is an alliance."

"I will not disagree with you."

Lady Catherine's mouth dropped open. It was clearly not the response she expected.

"Love can be a foolish thing, but do not dismiss something merely because it appears foolish. For love is not weak. It is not easily overcome." He knew full well how difficult it had been to try to overcome his love for Elizabeth – indeed, how foolish he had been to think he could overcome his love for Elizabeth. "And marriage is most assuredly an alliance. Between two hearts."

"That is not my meaning."

"I am well aware of that fact. I will not be moved."

"You are as stubborn as an old goat just like your uncle!" she cried. "What am I to do with Anne?"

Darcy shook his head. "I do not know."

Lady Catherine sighed and patted Dash's head, which was propped on her knee.

Darcy rose. "You will stay for at least the night, will you not?"

"Well, I am not returning to London at this hour of the day!"

"Then, it would be best if I were to introduce you to our host and hostess." Darcy stood at the door with his hand on the doorknob. "You will not disparage them."

Lady Catherine lifted her chin. "It goes without saying."

"Not a foul word about my betrothal will leave your lips?"

Her eyes narrowed, and she pouted very much like a petulant child would.

"Not a foul word," Darcy repeated.

His aunt's features relaxed as she affixed a smile on her lips. "It goes without saying. I am, of course, delighted for you."

Her voice was dripping with contempt, but it would have to do.

"Since I have your word." Darcy opened the door.

"You would not do this to me, would you?"

The softly spoken comment was met with a bark.

"That is a good boy," Lady Catherine whispered.

Darcy sighed and shook his head. Apparently, if a person were in the least bit difficult, his dog would befriend them and follow them to the gates of hell and back if asked.

Chapter 7

"I trust you slept well, Aunt Catherine?" Darcy looked up from the paper he was reading.

"Quite," she said as she took a seat to break her fast as she always did with a cup of tea, an egg, and a dry piece of toast.

Darcy had seen to it that the footmen assigned to the breakfast room were aware of his aunt's desires. She would not be toasting her own bread, nor did she expect to have to ask to be served.

"That cat," Lady Catherine's eyes followed Oliver as he slinked around the room, "has stolen my bracelet twice. He is not to be trusted."

"He also likes to pounce upon the table," Darcy cautioned. "However, I do believe you will be safe with Dash at your side. Oliver has yet to warm to Dash."

"Where is your sister?"

"She will likely be down soon. I believe she is expecting callers within the hour."

Hopefully, his aunt could be gone before the Bennets arrived. He did not need a repeat of last evening. It had been a struggle for him to endure his aunt's cutting, veiled remarks which did a poor job of disguising her displeasure even if they did not fall on the side of being disparaging — or, more precisely, they had ceased to fall on the side of being disparaging after Darcy had asked Bingley if the empty room above the stable might be readied. That had caused Lady Catherine to hold her tongue long enough for them to all retire for the night. However, this morning, there were no demeaning accommodations to use as a deterrent to his aunt's words. She could be sent away, but likely not before she could do some damage.

"Is there no meat in this house?"

"You do not eat meat for breakfast," Darcy said, peering up once again from his paper.

"You," she called to one of the footmen, "fetch me a small bit of ham if there is any." She turned her attention back to scraping the darkest crumbs from her toast. "Georgiana seems in good spirits."

"She is."

"Is there news of Richard in the paper?"

"Nothing in particular," Darcy replied.

"She is recovering well, then?"

"Georgiana?"

"Yes, of course, of whom else might I be speaking?" Lady Catherine cut her toast into four pieces as a plate with a slice of ham was placed on the table next to her. "Ah, that is just the thing. I was about to despair of anything proper being available in this place." She waved her knife in a circle in the air as she said *this place*.

"Netherfield is a fine estate and is run well. Mrs. Nichols is an excellent housekeeper, and Mr. Barrett excels at his post as well."

Lady Catherine pursed her lips and shook her head. "The servants can only be as good as their master, and their master," she waved her knife in the direction of the footmen, "knows little of how a master of an estate should conduct himself. No separation after the meal!"

"There was little need of separating," Darcy repeated what he had told her last night when she had voiced her displeasure over the *neglect of proper decorum*.

"There is always a need." She had finished cutting the ham into small pieces and, reaching over to take a fork from Darcy's place setting, she speared a morsel and fed it to Dash.

"He is not to be fed from the table!" Darcy cried.

"He is hungry. Just look at his eyes."

"He is a trickster," Darcy replied.

"He is a hungry trickster. Are you not?" Lady Catherine said to Dash as she fed him a second piece of ham. "That is all for the moment. I must eat my egg, and then you shall have some more."

"Good morning," Georgiana greeted as she entered the room.

"Your brother said you are expecting guests."

"I am expecting friends," Georgiana corrected.

"Friends? Here?"

Georgiana nodded as she accepted a cup of tea. "Miss Lydia, Miss Kitty, and Miss Mary promised to accompany their sisters to Netherfield today. There is a piece of music we wish to play and a dance to practice. I must be ready for my come out next season, you know."

"Indeed, you must." Lady Catherine scrutinized Georgiana as she ate the egg she had told Dash she was going to eat.

Dash pawed at her chair leg but returned to sitting attentively when Lady Catherine gave him a stern look before returning her attention to her niece.

Her brow arched, and her lips curled into a small smirk.

"Do you wish for your carriage to be readied?" Darcy asked. He did not like the calculating look on his aunt's face.

She shook her head. "I assume Miss Elizabeth Bennet is one of these young ladies' sisters?"

"Yes," Georgiana replied with a smile. "They are very pleasant."

Lady Catherine's right brow rose, imperiously this time, as her chin lifted.

"Your carriage?" Darcy tried once again.

"I will call for it when I am ready." She speared another piece of ham for Dash. "I think it would be best if I met this Miss Elizabeth since my brother has not yet exerted himself to do so."

"You will behave," Darcy cautioned.

"Perfectly," Lady Catherine said, lifting her cup to take a sip of tea. "Good morning, Sir Matthew, Miss Bingley."

She was being altogether too pleasant, and it made Darcy excessively uneasy, for Darcy knew that his aunt was rarely pleasant without a reason – or rather, a scheme to put in play. However, she gave no indication as to what the scheme might be while she and Dash finished their breakfast.

Upon leaving the breakfast room, Darcy sought out Mr. Barrett.

"Have Lady Catherine's carriage ready at a moment's notice," he instructed.

He needed to be prepared. He had warned his aunt that he would brook no disparagement of his betrothed, and while he did not fully expect her to blatantly ignore him, he also did not entirely trust her.

~*~*~

"So, you are the young woman who has finally turned Darcy's head?" Lady Catherine said after Darcy had made all the introductions when the Bennets arrived a quarter hour later.

"I suppose I am," Elizabeth replied.

"You are pretty."

"Thank you."

"There are a lot of you."

"Aunt," Darcy growled.

"It is a fact. I do not think I have seen five daughters all at once in one room," she said in defense of her comment.

"How is your father?" Bingley asked.

"He was in his study with a book when we left," Elizabeth replied.

"He seems more comfortable each day," Jane added.

"I am glad to hear it," Bingley said.

"Is your father not well?" Lady Catherine arranged herself in a chair that was close to the sofa on which Georgiana and the three youngest Bennets sat.

"Have you not heard?" Lydia asked as she scratched Dash's head. "He fell when touring Darcy House and broke his leg."

The information was met with a gasp of surprise from Lady Catherine.

"Dash tripped him," Darcy added.

"Dash did?"

The question was said with a great deal of surprise that Dash could ever do such a thing. Apparently, it did not matter that the animal had tried to do the very same thing to her yesterday on her arrival. Darcy thought to mention such to her, but it would likely not do any good.

"You really need to take him in hand, Darcy. One cannot have one's animal injuring people."

"I agree."

"As you should," Lady Catherine added.

"He has been learning to behave better," Lydia assured Lady Catherine. "He listens particularly well to Colonel Fitzwilliam and me. Actually," Lydia tipped her head, "that is not true. Dash listens well to me."

"Oh," was all Lady Catherine had to say in reply.

Lydia gasped. "I nearly forgot." She pulled a letter from her reticule. "I have had another letter." She rose and crossed to give the missive to Darcy. "Do not read the last paragraph," she whispered.

"Why is she giving you her mail?" Lady Catherine demanded.

"It is from his cousin," Lydia replied.

Darcy cringed at the admission. Lydia was far too trusting.

"Which cousin?"

"Colonel Fitzwilliam, my lady," Lydia said before resuming her seat.

"Fitzwilliam is writing to you?"

Darcy groaned.

"He has her father's permission," he interjected.

"How old are you?"

"Aunt," Darcy cautioned with a pointed look.

"I must know what sort of lady has captured my nephew's interest."

"I will be sixteen in April, my lady."

"Sixteen?" Shock suffused Lady Catherine's features. "And your father encourages this?" She waved at the missive Darcy held. "You are out before your sisters are married?"

"Elizabeth and Jane shall marry before me." Lydia looked at Darcy, confusion etched in her features.

"Things are not done now as they once were," Darcy added with a small smile for Lydia.

"I should say not!" Lady Catherine cried. Then, with a huff — a very displeased huff — she rearranged herself in her chair as if keeping to her seat were a great trial. "Marrying where you choose, rather than thinking of your family." She shook her head. "My brother might approve of you choosing as you have, Darcy, but I am certain he will not approve of *her* for his son!" Completely overcome and not being able to resist her restlessness a moment longer, she rose from her place.

"Why would he not?" Lydia asked.

"Why would he not?" Lady Catherine's eyebrows rose high, and she looked at Lydia as if the girl was the stupidest person she had ever met. "You ask why an earl would not approve of a lady of little means whose mother is from trade? Have you no sense of propriety?"

"He loves me," Lydia said above Dash's growl.

"You are not good enough for him," Lady Catherine snapped.

Dash positioned himself in front of Lydia and barked, startling Lady Catherine.

Lydia rose, arms folded, and eyes flashing. "I think that if Colonel Fitzwilliam is intelligent enough to lead a division of men, he is capable of choosing whom he wishes to marry," she spat.

"It is not done. The son of an earl marrying someone with ties to trade?" She shook her head. "The world has turned on its head. Darcy marrying beneath his sphere? A tradesman's son becoming a gentleman? A baronet marrying a tradesman's daughter? It is not proper."

"You might wish to speak to Lady Jersey about that," Sir Matthew inserted from the corner where he sat. "Her grandfather was a banker, you know. However, I imagine he would likely agree with you since he found an earl to be less than acceptable for his daughter. And I am also certain he is not the first to think in such a fashion." Sir Matthew paused for a moment as the room sat in silence. "It seems the world has been turned on its head for some time."

"Your carriage is waiting," Darcy said softly, taking his aunt by the elbow and moving her toward the door.

"It is not right," she protested as she left the room. "This is not how things are supposed to be."

"But it is how things are," Darcy said firmly. "And if you wish to continue visiting me, you will learn to accept them as they are. I have warned you. I will abide no disparagement of my betrothed or her family. Think on that carefully as you return to town. My mother would be saddened to think you had cut yourself off from me."

"But it is not my doing," Lady Catherine protested.

"It is entirely your doing, for it is your choice," Darcy said as Mr. Barrett handed Lady Catherine's wrap and hat to her.

"But she is..."

"My sister."

Lady Catherine's eyes grew wide at Darcy's declaration.

"And I will protect her just as I would Georgiana." He waited for his aunt to say something for she looked as if she wished to, but she remained silent. "May your journey be pleasant," he added, and then with a bow, he took his leave of her.

Chapter 8

Elizabeth kept one eye on her youngest sister and one eye on the door to Netherfield's drawing room. Lydia was sitting sullenly on the sofa. She had uncrossed her arms so that she could scratch Dash's ear, but her scowl still remained.

"That was vicious."

Elizabeth's eyes flicked in astonishment toward Caroline, the source of the whispered comment.

"There are people in this world who think they are better than others and are not sensible enough to keep their ignorance to themselves."

Caroline's head dipped at Sir Matthew's words, and a tinge of pink stained her cheeks.

"To think she thought you unfit to be my wife," Sir Matthew continued. "Utter balderdash is what it is."

Lydia brushed at the corner of her eye.

"Oh, there you are!" Bingley rose quickly from his seat and managed to capture Oliver before he could find a safe hiding place. "This is Oliver," he announced to the room.

Lydia's scowl softened to interest, and Elizabeth sighed in relief. There would likely still be some pouting and tears – how could there not be? Elizabeth was certain she would be a jumbled mess of emotions if she had been attacked in such a fashion as Lydia had been.

"He is a gift for Miss Bennet," Bingley continued.

"For me?" Jane's face lit with delight as Bingley handed Oliver to her. "Oh, he is beautiful." She made a small clicking sound to capture Oliver's attention before scratching him on the head and then stroking along his back. He stood on her lap and arched his back toward her hand.

"I acquired him before you arrived back at Longbourn," Bingley explained as he once again took a seat next to Jane. "Do you truly like him?" He scratched Oliver's head.

"He is perfect," Jane cooed.

Darcy entered the room just then, and Elizabeth shifted her attention from how her sister was playing with Oliver to him. He smiled at her but did not come to her side. Instead, he crossed to where his sister and hers were seated.

"Do you like kittens?" he asked Lydia, who nodded.

He bent to scratch Dash's ear. "We best not tell this fellow, or he will think he has lost his place."

A pleased and amused smile spread across Lydia's face.

"I will say I thought he might bite my aunt for a moment, which she would have rightly deserved."

Lydia's smile faltered.

"He is very loyal to you," Darcy added.

"He is."

"So is my cousin."

Elizabeth barely heard the whispered words which Darcy spoke as he once again scratched Dash's ear before turning his head to look at his sister.

"Were you going to practice some music, Georgiana?"

"We were," Georgiana answered. "Shall we go to the music room?" She rose.

"I think I should like that very much," Darcy agreed. "And you might even persuade me to join in the dancing if Miss Elizabeth will stand up with me."

Elizabeth nodded. She would follow him to the ends of the earth if he asked. He was crouched down now in front of Lydia, giving Dash another scratch.

"I will return your letter to you as soon as I have read all but the last paragraph," he assured her before standing and offering her his hand to aid in rising from her chair. "And," he said when she was on her feet and before he released her hand so she could join the others, "remember what my cousin said before he left Darcy House. He has made his choice and will not be dissuaded from it."

Lydia's lips curled into a small smile while her eyes glistened with tears as she nodded and whispered a quick "thank you."

While Lydia scooted from the room, Darcy's shoulders lifted and lowered as he drew and released a deep breath. "I cannot apologize for my aunt enough," he said to those who remained in the room. "There is not one of us who she did not censure." He shook his head. "I knew she would not be happy to hear of my betrothal, but I had not considered how she might respond to Miss Lydia."

"You could not know with certainty," Sir Matthew said. "She might come to her senses now that you have tossed her from the house."

Darcy chuckled. "I did not precisely toss her from the house."

"You escorted her out the door rather quickly," Bingley said.

Darcy shook his head and chuckled softly. "Very well, I did tell her that she will not be welcome to visit me if she continues as she has been. I will brook no disparagement of any member of my family."

"Which is as it should be," Sir Matthew agreed, although his eyes were on his betrothed.

Caroline fidgeted with the seam of her skirt and, without lifting her eyes from her hands, said, "Sir Matthew is correct. You should not abide any condemnation of those you love." She blew out a breath. "I must apologize for the times I have been that small person."

Her eyes finally lifted to look at her companions when no one spoke. She shrugged. "I wanted what I could not have." She straightened her shoulders. "I believe that is all I wish to say on that for now."

Sir Matthew captured her hand, and she smiled.

"Well, I will say this bit more," Caroline continued. "Though I mean no offense to Mr. Darcy, I think what I have received is far better than what I sought, and I have no desire to become a bitter lady such as your aunt."

It was perhaps not worded in the most appropriate fashion, but Darcy still smiled and accepted her apology with grace.

"I for one, am happy to hear it," Bingley said. "You may thank me later, dear sister."

"Thank you? For what?"

"To begin with, for allowing Sir Matthew to marry you."

Caroline gasped. "Allowing? Forcing is more like the truth!"

"Do you truly feel forced to marry me?" Sir Matthew asked.

Caroline's eyes narrowed, and her lips pressed into a thin line. "No," she admitted reluctantly.

"Then," Sir Matthew continued, "I think your brother is right in expecting a thank you at some point. I know I have thanked him several times for my good fortune." The gentleman lifted her hand to his lips, causing Caroline to smile.

"Very well. You are right as you often are," Caroline replied. "I shall have to thank you sometime, Brother. However, I do not think it will be today."

Darcy shook his head while chuckling softly to himself as he extended his hand to Elizabeth. "I believe we are expected in the music room."

"That was..."

"Surprising," Darcy finished Elizabeth's whispered sentence as he tucked her hand in the crook of his arm. "That man is a marvel."

"He is," Elizabeth said as she cast a look over her shoulder at the two couples remaining in the drawing room. Caroline was asking Jane something about a wedding breakfast. "I had worried about Jane having such a sister, but I do not think I need to worry any longer."

She rested her head against Darcy's shoulder as they ambled down the hallway. She had missed quiet moments with him like this. There had been many in the weeks she had been at Darcy House and few since her return to Longbourn.

"But then, I had also worried about my mother and sisters driving you to distraction, and I was wrong about that as well."

"They still might," Darcy admitted.

Elizabeth's cheek rubbed against the fabric of his

jacket as she shook her head. "You were wonderful with Lydia just now. Even if they do set your teeth on edge from time to time as they might – for they do mine – I have no reason to worry because I know you will handle it with great aplomb."

Music filtered through the door before them.

He smiled down at her and shook his head. "I cannot guarantee that I will not ever respond inappropriately, but I have promised you that I will endure it all because I love you."

Elizabeth peeked down the hall. The door to the drawing room was closed, and no servants were about. "And how will you assure me of your promise, sir?" she asked impertinently as she looked up into the eyes of the most wonderful man in the world.

A smile spread across his face, and he answered as she hoped he would by lowering those smiling lips to hers and wrapping her in his embrace.

Chapter 9

"Come in, my dears," Mr. Bennet called from his chair near the small hearth in his study as Elizabeth opened the door. "How many daughters are visiting me today?" He peeked over his shoulder toward the door. "My favourites," he said with a smile.

"No, Papa. I am here, too," Lydia said.

"And you are not my favourite youngest daughter? Have you given that position to Kitty? I shall have to write this down, so I do not forget if you have." He closed his book and tucked it between his leg and the arm of the chair.

"Oh, Papa," Jane chided. "You do not have favourites."

"Oh, but he does," Lydia replied. "You and Lizzy."

"Yes," her father said. "Jane is my favourite eldest daughter. Lizzy is my favourite second daughter. Mary is, of course, my favourite middle daughter. And then there is Kitty who is my favourite almost youngest daughter, and then there is you, my dear Lydia, who is and, I hope, shall always remain, my favourite youngest daughter."

"No," Lydia protested, "I am Mama's favourite, and Jane and Lizzy are your favourites. Poor Mary and Kitty are not favourites at all; except, Kitty and I are very good friends so perhaps she is my favourite." Lydia sighed and shook her head. "Poor Mary," she murmured. "It must be dreadful to be so alone."

Mr. Bennet's left eyebrow had quirked in question during Lydia's recital of how things were. "I believe," he said, "that a daughter might be favoured by both parents and her sisters and still not have exhausted the number of people to whom she is dear."

"Do you think so?" Lydia took a seat on a footstool next to Jane.

"I am certain of it," her father replied.

"But you cannot have *everyone* as your favourite. That is not how favourites work," Lydia declared.

"Which is nearly what I said," Jane inserted.

"Papa does not truly have favourites as you would think of favourites. He loves us all. It is just that there are particular things about each of us that endears us to him."

"Jane is a very wise young lady," Mr. Bennet said. "I have had my fun teasing you about favourites and trying to befuddle your mind with going in circles and will agree with Jane. She has said it perfectly."

"As she always does," Elizabeth said with a little laugh.

"Not always," Jane argued, though she grinned broadly while her eyes sparkled with amusement.

Lydia seemed either to have missed or to have chosen to ignore Elizabeth's and Jane's playful exchange. Her face was overwritten with curiosity.

"You like something particular about me?" Lydia asked her father.

He nodded. "I do."

"What?'

Her father steepled his fingers and rested his chin on them as he studied her for a moment in silence. "More than any of your sisters, you are the very image of your mother. How could I not admire that about you, for as you know from our time in

London, I love your mother very dearly. I always have, and I always will."

Elizabeth could not agree more with any of what her father said. Since spending time with Lydia at Sally's and hearing a portion of the story about their parents' courtship, Elizabeth knew just how much her parents loved each other and had come to realize just how much Lydia was like her mother. Sally had pointed it out many times, and Elizabeth had considered it in that moment and for several days afterward. However, she also knew that Lydia was not just a copy of her mother. Lydia also possessed her own special qualities. Qualities which were being drawn out and revealed because of Colonel Fitzwilliam.

"Now," her father said, "tell me about Netherfield. Does it still look as it did? Did you dance as you expected?"

Lydia nodded her head. "We did."

Mr. Bennet's brow furrowed. "That is all the report you have? Did you not see Dash? Am I to wonder about all the fixtures and furnishings?"

"Oh!" Lydia exclaimed. "Mr. Bingley gave Jane a kitten. His name is Oliver – not Mr. Bingley's. Oliver is the kitten's name."

"I did not bring him home." Jane's cheeks were rosy. "I thought it best that he stays in the home he knows for now."

"It will be her home eventually anyway," Lydia added as if no one in the room would remember that Jane was to marry Bingley. "Dash is not fond of Oliver, although I think he is merely curious about him and would really like to be his friend, but Oliver is so young. It really is not to be expected that Oliver would understand how to be a friend to Dash just yet."

"Well, that is well-thought out," muttered their father.

Elizabeth bit back a giggle at his perplexed expression.

"Mr. Darcy's aunt was there," Jane said quietly.

Lydia shook her head and looked sternly at her eldest sister. It was an action that did not go unnoticed by their father.

"She is no longer there," Elizabeth said.

"Mr. Darcy sent her away," Jane added. "She is not at all nice. In fact, she is very much like Mrs. Salter if you were to ask me." Jane's chin lifted. "She had not one nice word to say about anyone.

We are all beneath her notice, and therefore, we should also be beneath Mr. Darcy's notice."

"Indeed?" Mr. Bennet's brows were lifted high in surprise.

"Lady Catherine is Lord Matlock's sister," Elizabeth said. "We are, I suppose, beneath her, though I am loathed to admit it, for she was dreadful."

"And what do you think of her?" Mr. Bennet asked Lydia.

"I quite hope the wheels fall off her carriage, and I never have to see her again."

"I must say that is a bit excessive, do you not think?" her father exclaimed.

Lydia shook her head. "Not at all. She was most rude to me."

Mr. Bennet looked to his eldest daughters for confirmation of what Lydia had said. Both Jane and Elizabeth nodded their agreement.

"I was so excited to see Georgiana – I mean Miss Darcy – when I arrived at Netherfield that I quite forgot to give my letter to Mr. Darcy until we were all seated. And then when I did, Lady Catherine," Lydia's lips curled in displeasure as she said the name, "demanded to know why I had a letter from the colonel and was not at all pleased to hear he was writing to me with permission from you. She said dreadful things, and then Mr. Darcy made her leave." Lydia pulled her lip between her teeth as a crease formed between her eyes. "Do you think it might be acceptable for me to ask Miss Darcy or Miss Bingley to teach me how to act as a lady does in London and how to manage an estate as large as Netherfield?"

The room fell silent for a minute until their father cleared his throat and began by saying, "I would rather you learn to act as Miss Darcy or Jane does. They are far better examples of how ladies with any amount of true character should behave, and I would, therefore, have you behave as they do rather than how some lady in town is supposed to comport herself. I have very little use for the likes of many of the ladies I have met from town." He blew out a breath. "As for the management of an estate, there is none better than your mother to teach you what you will need to know –"

"But she will not allow me to do things. She will do them for me," Lydia pleaded.

"As I was saying," her father continued. "There is none better than your mother to teach you what you will need to know; however, if you feel that you could learn more from Miss Bingley or Miss Darcy, I shall write the request myself."

Lydia's eyes grew wide as did her smile. "Do you mean it?" she asked eagerly.

Her father nodded. "Whether I like it or not, I will have to give you away at some point, and I would not like to think you would go to your new home feeling inadequately prepared."

Lydia leapt from her seat, crossed to her father, and threw her arms around his neck. "Thank you, Papa. Thank you."

"You will behave as a proper student should, will you not?" He asked as he held her close.

"I absolutely will," Lydia assured him. "I just do not wish to be..." she stopped speaking, released his neck, and moved to return to her seat.

However, her father caught her hand and kept her by his side. "What do you not wish to be?"

Lydia darted a look at Jane and then Elizabeth before looking down at her slippers. "Not good enough," she whispered.

"Not good enough for what?" Mr. Bennet's voice was filled with incredulity as were his eyes.

"For the colonel," Lydia whispered.

"Has he said that?" Mr. Bennet demanded. There was no missing the anger in his voice.

Lydia shook her head violently. "He would never!"

"Then who said my daughter was not good enough?"

Elizabeth was uncertain if she had ever heard her father's tone be so cold.

"Lady Catherine," Jane answered for Lydia since Lydia seemed only able to shake her head but could not form the words needed to answer.

Lydia wiped her cheek quickly.

"Oh, my dear daughter." Mr. Bennet grasped Lydia's hand between both of his. "You are now more like your mother than even I ever expected you could be." He waited until her eyes lifted to his before he continued. "There were several who claimed that your mother was not good enough for me, but do you know who is the only one who can prove those people right or wrong?"

He pointed to himself. "Me. I am the only one who can say if your mother is or is not good enough for me – which she is, of course — and the colonel is the only one who can decide if you are good enough for him — which I believe is something he has already decided. However, I understand your worry, and I will write your request to Miss Darcy and Miss Bingley tonight and have it sent tomorrow." The right corner of his lips tipped up into a half smile. "I also quite wish for the wheels to fall off Lady Catherine's carriage. My daughter not good enough for the gentleman who loves her? I think not. The idea is quite preposterous." He released Lydia's hand and allowed her to go back to her seat. "Do not tell your mother about Lady Catherine unless you must."

"Why?" Elizabeth asked.

"She may go remove the wheels from Lady Catherine's carriage herself if she were to hear of it."

"She would not!" Jane cried as they all giggled at the thought.

~*~*~

Sometime later, after the intricacies of Miss Darcy's new piece of music had been explained and both Jane and Lydia had left their father's study, Mr. Bennet looked up from his book.

"I have not done my best by her."

Elizabeth stopped reading.

"That conversation we had in the Johnson's ballroom keeps coming back to me." He blew out a breath. "Will you help Lydia find her feet? She has never lacked for confidence before now, but I can see how it is possible since her education has not been what yours was. Do I ask too much?"

"No. No. Of course not. I will gladly help Lydia, as will Jane," Elizabeth assured her father.

He sighed as if a great weight had been relieved. "Would you do one more thing for me?"

"Of course."

"Would you call someone to help me to my room? My leg is aching a bit more today than yesterday, and I fear it is because I attempted to do too much."

Elizabeth closed her book and assured her father that she would see that someone was sent to assist him as soon as possible.

It did not take long for her to find someone. Mr. Hill was just passing the study when she exited, and he sent a footman directly.

However, Mr. Bennet had only made it to the bottom of the staircase when there was a knock at the door.

"Might I speak with Mr. Bennet and Miss Elizabeth," Darcy said as he entered.

"You do not look well, sir," Mr. Bennet said.

"I am not," he answered. He held out a letter. "I have just received this and must be gone straight away."

Mr. Bennet motioned to the chair in the corridor and the footman assisted him in sitting. "I see," was all he said when he read the letter Darcy had handed him. "Of course, you must go to him."

"Who?" Elizabeth's heart was beating a rapid pace. Her father's expression was so grave, and Darcy was so distraught.

"My cousin," Darcy replied. "Richard has been injured most grievously."

Chapter 10

"I expect my carriage to be ready when I return to Netherfield," Darcy said as Elizabeth finished reading the letter he had received from one of Richard's fellow officers and had brought to Longbourn with him. They had gone to Mr. Bennet's study as instructed by Elizabeth's father so that Elizabeth might read the news in private, and so that Darcy might take his leave of his betrothed without an audience. For both of those things, Darcy was immensely grateful to Mr. Bennet.

"Will you travel through the night?" Elizabeth looked up at him from the letter, concern shimmering in unshed tears in her eyes.

Darcy nodded. "I must get to him as soon as can be."

"You will be careful, though?" She brushed at a tear which escaped her eye, and Darcy pulled her into his embrace. "It is bad enough that Colonel Fitzwilliam is injured. I do not need you to join him," she whispered against his coat.

"I will do all that is necessary to return to you, my love," he assured her before placing a kiss on the top of her head.

She held him tightly. "Where will you take him? He cannot remain in an inn where there is so much unrest. The noise of it all would not be conducive to his recovery, I am certain."

"Bingley suggested I bring him to Netherfield since it is close enough to town for my physician to attend him if needed and for my aunt and uncle to call on him since parliament is still sitting. It makes sense."

"And the air in the country is far better for someone who is unwell," Elizabeth added.

Darcy rubbed her back and relished these few moments of comfort, storing them in his memory to carry with him as he travelled to Manchester.

He knew only a few details about Richard's injury from the letter. There had been an attack at a mill, and in the tumult, his cousin had sustained several lacerations as well as a blow to the head that had rendered him insensible. The message had been sent two days ago, so whether his cousin had regained his senses or not was unknown. However, Darcy was attempting to prepare himself for the worst scenario.

Though he did not wish for Elizabeth to witness any of the trouble in the north or the gruesomeness of any injuries associated with it, Darcy yearned to be able to have the solace he found in her presence with him on his journey.

He sighed, knowing both that he must not remain here with her much longer and that he had one more task to complete before he could leave. "Your sister needs to be told," he said softly, "but I fear that I do not know how to tell her."

"We will tell her together," Elizabeth offered.

And they had.

Lydia had been surprisingly calm during the ordeal. She had cried, of course, but Darcy had expected her to be more vocal in her grief. She had always seemed so like Mrs. Bennet, who was boisterous. He shook his head at his foolishness as he shifted in his seat in his carriage. How often would he have to remind himself that what he expected from the Bennets was often not what he received? Had not Elizabeth and Jane, as well as their parents, already surprised him enough for him to have learned that his initial assessments of them had been wrong? Was it not possible for Lydia to have a more thinking nature buried beneath her effervescent exterior just as her sister, Jane, had a scheming mind tucked neatly behind a composed smile? People were, he reasoned, made of many layers. Having been often accused of being only severe and reserved, he should have a better understanding of these things. But apparently, he did not.

He sighed and propped his head against the squabs. He really did need to work on being more considerate of the many facets a person might possess rather than arrogantly assuming his first impression of a person was unwaveringly correct.

However, he would not ponder on that now. He would save it for later. For presently, he needed this journey to be completed quickly, and so, sleep was necessary. Travelling never seemed to take as long as it truly did when one slept for a portion of the time.

However, even sleeping as often as he could did not shorten the amount of time Darcy had to worry about his cousin or to miss Elizabeth during his trip. Two days of travel, broken only by the necessary stops to change horses had given him ample time to think about a great many things. Having finally reached Pemberley, he climbed out of his coach and stretched his back before giving an appreciative nod to his driver and making his way towards the house.

Mr. Jarvis, his butler, greeted him with Mrs. Reynolds at his side.

"All is ready," Mrs. Reynolds assured Darcy. "Your bath was drawn as soon as we heard you were at the gate, and your dinner will be in your sitting room within the half hour."

"And the room for Richard?"

"All is ready, sir. The surgeon will be waiting when you arrive with Colonel Fitzwilliam tomorrow evening."

"Thank you, Mrs. Reynolds." Darcy sighed softly as he began to climb the stairs to his room.

"He will be well." Mrs. Reynolds had apparently caught the sigh that had escaped Darcy. "We must believe that," she added when he glanced her direction.

"You are right, of course, Mrs. Reynolds. It is just not knowing what I will find tomorrow which has me troubled."

"That is understandable, sir."

Darcy continued on his way up the steps. A warm bath might help relieve some of the stiffness he felt from sitting in a carriage for two days, and a comfortable bed would not be an unwelcome luxury. Sleeping in a carriage – even one as well-sprung and richly upholstered as his was – was not conducive to feeling well-rested. Hopefully, the lack of proper rest would help him sleep well tonight.

And it did – eventually.

Darcy had lain in bed pondering life and its brevity for three-quarters of an hour before weariness claimed not only his body but his mind.

As the sun rose above the horizon the following day, Darcy woke with muscles that only ached a bit. He would take a short walk in the garden in an attempt to shake loose the remaining stiffness before climbing into his carriage today. Then he would collect his cousin and tomorrow, he would see his steward before he began the journey back to Netherfield. There was no point in being in residence even for a short time without checking on the state of his holdings.

Therefore, after his walk in the garden and

before he had eaten breakfast, a message was sent to Mr. Turner informing him of Darcy's wish to see him on the morrow. Then, after a filling breakfast, Darcy was once again on his way to Manchester.

Just over half a day later, Darcy exited his carriage and entered the inn where Richard had his lodgings.

"Who is there?" Richard barked from his bed.

Darcy breathed a sigh of relief, his cousin was alive and awake, even if he did sound to be in a disagreeable mood.

"Darcy," he said as he made his way toward the bed. "I have come to take you to Pemberley and then to Netherfield." He sucked in a breath as he took in the appearance of his cousin.

"I look a fright, do I not?" Richard grumbled. "Not that anyone will give me a mirror to see the surgeon's handiwork – no matter how much I have threaten."

"The surgeon's stitches are tidy." Darcy replied. "However, there are a great number of them. This is not the wound sustained in the altercation about which you wrote me earlier, is it?"

Richard attempted to move his head but

groaned and held his head still. "No. That is the cut above my left eye."

The large gash on his cheek was as fresh as it appeared.

Richard held out a hand. "If you do not mind, I could use some help in rising."

"Are you supposed to rise?" Darcy questioned. "I had thought someone was to carry you down for me. That is what I was told."

"I have two legs that still mostly work," Richard grumbled. "I can see myself to the carriage." He waved his hand at Darcy. "Now, help me rise." He winced and blew out a great breath as Darcy helped him to a sitting position. "Make sure there is ample brandy in the carriage, will you?" he ordered, a grimace still on his face.

Darcy knew that Richard's injuries were far more extensive than what could be seen above the collar of his nightshirt and robe. The fact that Richard was dressed as he was to travel was a sure sign that the rest of his body was not in a condition worthy of a uniform. Bandages were more easily covered by loose-fitting garments.

"There will be plenty of brandy. I will see to it,"

Darcy assured him. "Where are your other injuries?"

Richard placed a hand on his right side. "Here. My left shoulder is not in usable order. My left thigh also has a number of stitches, and of course, as you can see the once lovely features of my face have been marred." He squeezed his eyes shut. "And the room refuses to stay still." Again, he blew out a great breath.

"I have readied the carriage as best I can for your comfort, but I fear it will still not be a pleasant trip." Darcy took Richard's hand once again to help him rise, just as two officers arrived in the room.

"We are to see our colonel to his carriage," one of the men said.

Richard attempted to take a step toward them, but he stumbled as if he had miscalculated the distance between his foot and the floor and had expected the floor to be further beyond him than it was. He sucked in a sharp breath.

"My apologies," the officer on his right said. "I did not mean to cause you pain. I only wished to keep you from falling."

Richard nodded. "Do you think you could make the floor stand still? It is dashed hard to know where to place my foot." He turned his head to the left. "Oh, there you are, Darcy. I had thought you were gone. I did not see you."

"You did not see me?" Darcy asked in surprise. He was standing almost equal with Richard's left shoulder. He should have been visible to his cousin.

"My eyes are not right," Richard admitted. "The blow to the head, you see. We are hopeful that it will clear at the same time the room stops spinning and my head stops throbbing."

Slowly – much more slowly than Darcy had ever witness Richard walk – they made their way down the stairs and to the front of the inn, and after a word of parting to the innkeepers, Richard allowed the two officers who were on either side of him to help him into Darcy's carriage.

Chapter 11

"I beg your pardon?" Darcy turned from the window in Richard's room at Pemberley. The surgeon had left a half hour ago, and Darcy and Richard had been discussing Richard's time in Manchester.

"I am not going to Netherfield."

That was exactly what Darcy thought he had heard his cousin say, but it had startled him so much that he had to ask for it to be repeated. The surgeon had been impressed with the quality of care Richard had received and did not fear there would be any complications such as infection. The wounds were all clean and properly dressed. There was no need to remain at Pemberley. The surgeon had not thought it would be dangerous to attempt a longer trip.

"I have written to your father informing him that you will be at Netherfield," Darcy argued.

"You may write to him again. Tell him that I am well but prefer to rusticate in the country far removed from callers."

Darcy shook his head. Richard was not the sort to ever wish to rusticate in the country. That knock he had received on his head must have jiggled something loose.

"I can write to him myself as soon as the pen and paper agree to stay in the same place at the same time," Richard added.

Darcy crossed the room to sit in a chair closer to the bed. "It is not just your father who wishes to see you."

"Mother is welcome to come visit if she wishes to make the trip during the season." He had turned his face away from Darcy while he spoke.

"And I suppose Georgiana can travel with her?" Darcy asked incredulously.

"I am certain there would be room in Mother's carriage," Richard answered. "And I think I could tolerate the three of you." His head turned toward Darcy. "But no more."

Darcy sat quietly for several minutes studying the way his cousin held his jaw firmly in position and then taking note of the way the blanket over

Richard's chest rose and fell with deep, deliberate breaths.

"What of Lydia?" Darcy asked softly, breaking the silence but only for the length of time it took for him to utter the words.

Richard did not reply. He continued to breathe deeply as he stared up at the canopy above him.

"You cannot abandon her."

"She is young. She will find another."

Darcy leaned back in his chair. Something very close to anger rose within him.

"And what if she does not want another?" Darcy attempted to keep his voice from betraying his feelings. His cousin was injured and not thinking correctly. He did not deserve to feel the anger that Darcy felt at the thought of Lydia being injured in such a fashion as Richard was proposing.

"She will. Describe my appearance and tell her I am likely to lose my position in the regulars. I have little to offer her." Richard closed his eyes, but a tear escaped and ran down the side of his face toward his ear.

Allowing Richard to see himself in the mirror had been a mistake. Darcy had suspected it was at the time but had disregarded his better judgment in favour of satisfying his cousin's curiosity.

The scar on Richard's face ran the length of his cheek from nearly his ear to the almost the corner of his mouth, and it was an angry red presently with a track of neat stitches holding it closed. It looked horrid now, but it would not forever. It was going to scar, but it would fade somewhat with time.

Added to that his face was not what made him who he was. Not that Darcy could fault Richard for feeling as he did at the moment. Proper reasoning might return once some of the pain from his cousin's injuries subsided.

Darcy rose. There was little use arguing any of those things with Richard at present. It would be better to just inform him of what was going to happen and attempt to ignore his cousin's cursing and grumbling.

"I will do nothing of the sort," Darcy said. "We are going to Netherfield tomorrow."

"I am not going," Richard yelled at the back of his cousin's retreating form.

Darcy turned from the door and went to stand beside Richard's bed. "You are going to Netherfield even if I have to contact the apothecary to acquire a potion to render you insensible."

There was no way as long as the sun still shone in the sky on a clear day that Darcy was going to allow his cousin to hide from life and lock his heart away.

"Perhaps that might be for the best anyway. It is not a short journey, and your injuries are not insignificant." He turned, once again, to leave the room.

"Why?"

The pain in Richard's tone kept Darcy from leaving, but he did not turn back to look at his cousin.

"Because Elizabeth is at Longbourn, and I will not allow you to separate me from her." If Richard was unable to care for his own heart at present, perhaps he would be able to care about Darcy's.

"Then go without me."

That would not keep Darcy from the desire of his heart, but it would do nothing for Richard's. It might be best to lay Richard's heart before him and let his cousin know that Lydia was important not only to Richard but also to Darcy.

"And," Darcy continued, "there is a young lady

at Longbourn who loves you and was excessively concerned for you when I told her about my need to collect you. I gave her my word that I would return to Netherfield *with you*, and to return without you would mean I would have to break my word to her. I will not do that to her just as I would not break my word to you or Georgiana. Therefore, since I refuse to either break my word to her or to break her heart at your request, we are going to Netherfield in the morning after I have seen my steward. I suggest you try to get as much rest tonight as is possible."

And with those words, Darcy left his cousin. He leaned against the wall outside Richard's door. An injured family member was a great worry, but when the happiness of both that family member and another hung precariously in the balance, the weight of it all was nearly too much to bear. How he missed Elizabeth and her comforting presence!

He pushed off the wall and headed to his study. A concoction to help Richard sleep during their journey was indeed a good idea. Therefore, a note needed to be sent to the apothecary.

He sighed. The note to the apothecary would be easily written. The other letter which must be sent would not be so easily done. Lydia needed to be informed about the extent of Richard's injuries. Darcy knew he could write directly to her. No one would think anything of it. However, there was the matter of Richard's refusal to return to Netherfield that weighed more heavily on Darcy than any scar or loss of uniform. And because of that, he would write to Elizabeth. She would know how best to share all of this information with her sister.

"Mr. Jarvis," Darcy said when handing the missives he had written to his butler to be delivered, "my cousin is not in favour of leaving with me tomorrow. While I do not think he is well enough to manage such a feat as stealing away in the night, I prefer not to be surprised by his tenacity. Therefore, if you would inform those who need to know, that Colonel Fitzwilliam is not to be allowed to leave the house, and he is most certainly not to be given a horse or carriage for his use." It was unsettling to have to give such orders regarding his cousin. "Again, I do not expect him to attempt an escape, but I do wish to be prepared."

"It is the colonel, sir. I remember him as a boy. There is not much that could keep him from his plans."

Darcy chuckled. It was true. Richard had never been the sort to simply sit around and do as he was told.

Darcy thanked Mr. Jarvis for his understanding and then settled in a favourite chair in his study to read – or as it turned out, to look at a book with the pretense of reading while he pondered his cousin.

~*~*~

The next day, Richard glared at Darcy while Darcy attempted to ignore his cousin's displeasure at waking to find himself in the carriage. The potion the apothecary had delivered had worked well.

"Would you like another dose of medicine?" Darcy inquired.

"You know that I do not," Richard snapped. "I would like to be in a comfortable bed rather than this carriage."

"As would I," Darcy agreed, shifting slightly to make himself more comfortable. The carriage had been fitted with a board and mattress so that Richard could sit without bending his legs and if he bent his knees, it was not entirely impossible to lie down. Lying down would help with the dizziness and give his shoulder and side more rest.

"Aunt Catherine called at Netherfield the day before I received news of your injury." That bit of news should distract Richard from his displeasure with Darcy, and likely place it with someone else.

"Why would she call on Bingley?"

As Darcy expected, Richard was too curious to let a disagreeable mood keep him from discovering what he wanted to know.

"She was calling on me. It seems Mrs. Collins – Mr. Collins is Elizabeth's cousin who is Lady Catherine's parson if you remember."

Richard assured Darcy that he remembered that fact before Darcy continued.

"As it happens, Mrs. Collins had a letter from her mother, Lady Lucas, who is a particular friend of Mrs. Bennet and in that letter was news of my betrothal to someone other than our cousin Anne."

Richard rubbed his chin as he let out a long, low whistle.

"Indeed," Darcy agreed. "She was not pleased to hear the news and even less pleased that your father would not support her in her desire to see me marry Anne."

"She went to my father first?"

Darcy nodded. "Do you know that Dash took an immediate liking to her?"

"To Aunt Catherine?" Richard cried incredulously.

Again, Darcy nodded. "Well, that is he liked her right up until she spoke harshly to his Miss Lydia. Then, he asserted himself on Miss Lydia's behalf."

The sound of carriage wheels and horse's hooves were the only thing heard inside Darcy's travelling coach for a full minute before Richard asked what Darcy expected.

"Aunt Catherine spoke harshly to Miss Lydia?"

For a third time, Darcy nodded.

"About what?"

"You."

Richard's brow furrowed.

"Miss Lydia had just received a letter from you and gave it to me to read when she arrived at Netherfield." He looked Richard in the eye. "Apparently, Miss Lydia is not good enough for the son of an earl."

Anger flashed in Richard's eyes just as Darcy hoped it would.

"I assured Miss Lydia that you were not inconstant," Darcy continued. "I do hope I have not misspoken."

Again, the carriage fell silent. Darcy pretended to attend to his book while surreptitiously studying his cousin who was clearly battling a mix of emotions.

"I also told Aunt Catherine that she was not welcome in my home if she were to continue to speak poorly of one of my sisters, and then, I sent her back to your father."

Richard's eyes grew wide.

"Have you not spoken to your father about Miss Lydia?" Darcy asked in surprise.

"No. I was going to write to him about her. There was not time to speak to him before I left town." He blew out a breath. "I suppose he must know by now."

"Most likely. Aunt Catherine is not one to keep news such as that to herself."

Richard groaned.

"Would you like some medicine now?" Darcy asked with a grin.

"No, but if you have some brandy, I will not refuse it."

Chapter 12

Lydia was sitting in the garden on the same bench she had sat on for each of the days since she had heard of Colonel Fitzwilliam's injury. From that bench, Elizabeth knew that Lydia could see the drive, and, therefore, she could see who was or was not arriving. At least, today, Lydia's good friend, Maria Lucas, had joined her while, in Longbourn's sitting room, their mothers discussed all the dreadful possibilities that might be the result of any injury sustained in battle.

"Might we go out as well?" Georgiana asked as she joined Elizabeth near the window.

"I must apologize for my mother's choice of topic for discussion," Elizabeth whispered. "Did you and Kitty have as much time to practise as you wished?"

Georgiana wore a pleased smile as she nodded.

"Kitty is almost able to play that song without a single stumble."

The pride of accomplishment mingled with the joy of hearing oneself praised in Kitty's expression. "I have never played anything so well, to be honest."

Georgiana had been accompanying Bingley each day when he came to call on Jane. She and Kitty would find some excuse to not be in the sitting room. On one day, they had read lines from a play, on another day, they had pored over fashion magazines while examining the content of Kitty's wardrobe to see what alterations could be made to various dresses to make them more fashionable, and today, they had spent time working on a song Kitty wished to learn to play and sing.

Mrs. Bennet's voice had dropped to a whisper when Georgiana had entered the sitting room, but even when whispering Mrs. Bennet's voice carried.

"It is a true marvel what a bit of practice can do," Elizabeth teased. "Perhaps one day I shall try it." She wrapped one arm around Kitty's and the other around Georgiana's. "But I have no desire to practise today. The sun is warm, and I think Georgiana's suggestion to join Lydia is a very good one."

The three young ladies exited the sitting room and gathered their things to go to the garden. Just as they were starting down the path to where Lydia sat, she jumped up and, after a hasty word to her friend, ran toward the front of the house.

Elizabeth hurried to Maria. "What is it?"

"An express rider," Maria said, pointing to the front of the house.

"It is for Elizabeth," Lydia cried, waving the missive in the air.

"For me?" Elizabeth went to meet her sister. Taking the letter, she looked at the address and then, with a smile, broke the seal.

"What does it say?" Lydia asked anxiously. "Has Mr. Darcy seen his cousin?"

"He misses me."

"Yes, yes. But what of his cousin?" Lydia was wringing her hands and pacing in front of the bench on which she had been sitting as Elizabeth took a seat and continued to read.

"Oh! I can tell by your face it is not good," Lydia cried. "Will he live?"

"He is not in danger of dying," Elizabeth assured her. "However..." she paused. How was she supposed to share this information with her sister?

Darcy had far more faith in her abilities to do so than she did herself. However, he had entrusted her with this news, and she would see it done. She placed the letter in her lap and, leaned forward to grasp Lydia's hand. "Sit with me."

Lydia did as she was told.

Elizabeth picked up the letter once more and scanned its content. Her protective nature told her to only reveal the bits and pieces that would not be too distressing while her rational nature told her that doing so would only lead to a greater possibility of being hurt later.

"If the colonel were to ask you to marry him, would you?" Elizabeth asked.

"Yes," Lydia cried.

"Then you believe yourself capable of facing troubles as a grown lady should?" Elizabeth asked.

"I am not a child."

The pout that accompanied the words did little to convince Elizabeth of their truth, but she chose to ignore that thought.

"Very well. You may read the entire letter." Elizabeth handed it to Lydia but did not release it. "Of course, the parts about Mr. Darcy's love for me are not to be part of any gossip."

Lydia nodded, and Elizabeth released her hold on the letter.

"There are a few new plants beginning to push through the soil," Kitty said.

"Indeed?" Georgiana asked.

Kitty nodded. "I saw them yesterday. They were not more than a few green specks in the dirt. Would you and Maria like to join me to see how much they have grown between then and now?" She smiled at Elizabeth. "I am certain after Lydia has had a read of Mr. Darcy's letter, the news that needs to be told to us will be shared."

"I would not withhold any important information," Elizabeth assured them. "Thank you," she mouthed to Kitty as the three young ladies moved down the path.

"Mr. Darcy does love you very much," Lydia whispered.

"And he loves you as you will see by his concern." Lydia was about to read the account of the colonel's unwillingness to travel to Netherfield.

Lydia's hand flew to her chest. "Stay at Pemberley?"

Elizabeth rubbed her back.

"Find another? Not wish to marry him?" She

turned troubled eyes to Elizabeth. "How could he think such things?"

"How is not the right question," Elizabeth replied. "Why is the better choice."

Lydia brushed tears from her cheeks with the palm of her right hand while her left clutched the letter. Gently, Elizabeth took the letter from her and handed her a handkerchief.

"I will read this part to you."

Lydia nodded.

> *I cannot blame him for his troubled thinking, but I will not allow him to hide from his heart.*

Elizabeth put an arm around Lydia's shoulders and squeezed her close. "*You* are the colonel's heart," she whispered before continuing to read.

> *Therefore, I am bringing him to Netherfield whether he wishes it or not.*
>
> *When you see the state he is in; I am certain you, too, will understand his wish to remain in seclusion. He has several injuries. One of his injuries has rendered his left arm useless until it heals. He has several stitches to close wounds on his side and his upper leg. In addition to these things, he sustained an injury to his head that currently affects his eyesight. However, I do not*

believe any of those, save perhaps the head injury (which I will explain later), are the cause of his wish to hide.

It is his face. He has a small scar above his eye which we knew from one of his letters, as well as new large gash from his ear to his mouth on the right side of his face. It is, of course, bruised, red, and still being held closed by stitches. I will not lie to you or your sister. It looks as gruesome as you might imagine it. However, with time, it will heal.

He told me to describe this injury to your sister as an explanation of why she would not wish to marry him. In addition to that, he added that he might lose his position in the regulars. That is the part which has to do with the blow he received to his head. If his eyesight does not improve, he will not be fit to serve. He sees this as another reason why your sister might not wish to marry him.

Elizabeth peeked at Lydia who was shaking her head while silently crying.

He feels he has little to offer Miss Lydia. Little but his heart! Not that he is capable of seeing that at present. It is this knowledge that keeps me from truly being angry with him. As his body heals, so will his spirit.

I did not know how to impart such information to your sister, and so I am trusting you to inform her of these details as you see fit. My heart grieves both for her and Richard.

I am eager to see you, my love. Until I arrive at Netherfield, hold my sisters close and care for them for me.

"And that is all there is," Elizabeth pulled Lydia close again. "Mr. Darcy said to hold his sisters – *sisters* – close," she whispered. "He cares for you very much, Lydia."

Lydia nodded.

"As does his cousin. Such injuries would cause anyone to falter and think of themselves as not good enough."

"But he is," Lydia whispered. "He is good enough." She drew a deep breath through her nose and released it slowly through her mouth. "It is as Papa said. Colonel Fitzwilliam is not the person who gets to decide if he is good enough for me." She turned toward Elizabeth with a determined look in her eye. "Only I get to decide that."

"He will be scarred and not as handsome as he was, and he might not have a uniform any longer," Elizabeth cautioned, not because she wished to dissuade her sister from thinking the colonel was good enough but to test Lydia's resolve. A handsome gentleman in a uniform – the higher the rank, the better — had always been Lydia's ideal for who would make a good husband.

"I am not stupid," Lydia muttered.

"No, you are not, but will you feel cheated by his injuries? It would not be wrong to feel something about them."

Kitty, Georgiana, and Maria were making their way toward the house. Apparently, someone – likely Kitty – had decided they should not return to Elizabeth and Lydia at present. Elizabeth had to admit she was pleased to see such conscientiousness developing in Kitty. Kitty had not always considered much more than what Lydia's thoughts on a subject might be, or how something would make her look. However, it seemed all of Elizabeth's sisters were becoming grown women in more than just age and appearance.

She squeezed Lydia's shoulders once more. Who would have thought that Mr. Darcy, along with his cousin and sister, would be the one to work such miracles? She smiled as she thought of him standing at the edge of the assembly in the autumn, looking down his nose at everyone around him. How he had improved upon greater acquaintance!

"Are you ready to go in?" Elizabeth whispered.

Lydia rose, dried her eyes and nose once more, straightened her shoulders, and lifted her chin.

Elizabeth wound her arm around Lydia's, and they took their time returning to the house. Just as they were about to enter through the servant's entrance, Lydia stopped.

"I am scared," she whispered when Elizabeth turned toward her. "What if I am not as good as you or Jane?"

"What do you mean? Neither Jane nor I are better than you."

"Oh, you are!" Lydia cried. "You think about things that are not fashion."

"That does not make us better."

Lydia looked at the ground. "What if I discover I am not the kind of lady who can love someone who is not handsome?"

Elizabeth lifted Lydia's chin so that she could see her sister's eyes. "Do you think you are that sort of woman?"

Lydia nodded and then shrugged. "I do not

know. I have never flirted with anyone who was not handsome."

"You have flirted with Mr. Ferrell, and well, he is not particularly handsome. And you are kind to Miss King despite her freckles and plumpness."

A small smile tipped up the corner of Lydia's mouth. "That is true."

"If your heart is truly engaged with Colonel Fitzwilliam, you will not find his appearance to be of great significance." She smiled reassuringly at Lydia. "Of course, we will likely not know that until we have seen the colonel, but I have faith in you, Lydia. You are not the silly little sister you were. You are becoming a fine young woman."

"Do you really think so?" Lydia's eyes were wide with shock.

"I do. Now, Mama will want to know about the colonel as will Georgiana and Mr. Bingley."

"Oh, I cannot bear to face Mama," Lydia said.

"Then, I suggest you go tell Papa what you have heard while I tell the others."

Lydia stopped half in and half out of the house, holding the door open against her hip. "But you usually tell Papa everything."

Elizabeth tugged at Lydia to get her to enter the

house. "This time, I think he should hear it from you. Now, scoot. Before Mama comes looking for you."

Chapter 13

"Are you ready for this?" Elizabeth whispered the question to Lydia two days later as they waited for Netherfield's door to open to them.

Lydia nodded and smiled, but from the way her sister clung to her arm, Elizabeth was not so certain Lydia was prepared for her first lesson in estate management. How had she never noticed any sort of unease in Lydia before that dreadful night when they found themselves at Sally's house?

"You will do well," Jane encouraged.

Jane. She was the reason, Elizabeth supposed. Not that Jane was to blame. No. Elizabeth knew it was entirely her own fault that she had not paid closer attention to her youngest sister. She had always relied on Jane to see to what needed care. In that way, Elizabeth imagined herself to be somewhat like Kitty – relying on a favoured sister to guide her. Thankfully, Jane was a sensible sister, Elizabeth thought with a smile just as the door before them opened.

The three Bennet sisters followed the butler, Mr. Harvey, into the drawing room where Miss Bingley and Mrs. Nicholls, Netherfield's housekeeper, were waiting for them.

"I thought it best to begin with a tour," Caroline said after the pleasantries of greetings were completed. "Jane will, of course, need to see the house, and well," she smiled at Elizabeth, "it would be rather rude of me to exclude one of my guests."

"I can read in the library," Elizabeth suggested.

"No, no, I am only jesting. I am nearly over my dislike of you." Again, Caroline smirked.

Elizabeth was not certain if that remark was also said in jest or not.

"I am teasing," Caroline said. "I am capable of doing so – or, I should say, I am attempting to learn to do so. Sir Matthew insists that I try to be more at ease." She blew out a breath. "However, I am not certain that teasing puts me at ease."

"If one does not like to tease, then one should not feel compelled to do so," Lydia said. "I am not clever enough to tease as Lizzy does, and so, it feels very awkward. Some of us are just not made for things such as teasing."

Caroline's eyebrows rose and her lips pursed as she considered that thought. "I must say, Miss Lydia, that I believe you are correct. I think I am far too serious a lady to ever be very good at teasing. However, I am quite good at giving opinions while others stumble over a simple 'It is lovely.'"

Elizabeth bit the inside of her mouth to keep from laughing as she and Jane followed behind Caroline and Lydia. Miss Bingley was excessively good at sharing her opinion.

"You saw many of the public rooms when you were here for our ball in November," Caroline said to Lydia. "And Jane and Miss Elizabeth have seen some of the private quarters as they were guests here for several days. However, we will make a thorough inspection of all the rooms." She stopped in the corridor just outside the drawing room and turned back toward the door.

"You will notice that this room is bright and has a good amount of air in it due to its size. These things are important if you are to have a great number of callers at one time, which can happen. I have seen drawing rooms that were nearly overflowing in London, and some of them were not bright or airy, and the need for a nosegay became particularly strong as a result." She tipped her head and studied the room before her. "Of course, you will have someone to tend to the ashes in the fireplace and others to keep the surfaces of the tables shining as well as someone to see that the fabric and rugs are tidy. There is a door at the far end, do you see it? It is nearly obscured by design."

"Oh, yes! It is very cleverly done," Lydia answered.

"That is how your servants will most often enter and exit. Well, the junior staff and below, that is. Servants such as Mrs. Nicholls and Mr. Harvey will enter just as we do. There are lines which must not be crossed. Order cannot be retained as it should be if any maid or groom is allowed to come flouncing in however he or she wishes." She smiled at Jane. "That is my opinion, of course. A mistress of an estate must determine with the agreement of her husband as to how those lines are formed and how firmly they are held. Sir Matthew, I believe, is more forgiving of things than I am, and, therefore, I shall have to learn his ways." She turned from the room and took Lydia's arm. "One must always consider the opinion of one's husband to be the greater opinion."

"But what if he is wrong?" Lydia asked.

"He is not. Ever."

"I think it is not impossible for a husband to be wrong," Sir Matthew said from where he stood on the grand staircase. "However, I try not to be wrong too often." He bowed his good days to the ladies. "Not every rule which is parroted from matron to daughter must remain as it is. It is my opinion, that a good marriage is a friendship of the greatest kind. The joining of two people to act as one – not to become as the other but to enhance and support the other." He smiled and shrugged. "My father was a parson. I fear I have picked up some of his ability to wax eloquent on some subjects which interest me. However, I shall attempt to keep my thoughts to a minimum as I should allow you to return to your tour. I was just on my way to the library."

"To read?" Lydia asked.

"Yes," Sir Matthew replied, his lips twitching ever so slightly.

"Will you be there long?"

He nodded. "Most likely, unless something draws me away from my book."

"I only ask," Lydia said very seriously, "so that I will know to be quiet when I enter. My father does not like to be disturbed when he is reading, you see."

Sir Matthew gave a small bow of his head. "I thank you in advance for your consideration." He looked at Caroline. "You are doing an admiral job, my dear."

Caroline beamed as she watched him make his way to the library. "I have been blessed." She sighed but then looked at Jane. "Even if I did not think it a blessing at first, it is."

Jane blushed. "We selected him only because we thought he would make you happy," she said softly.

"We?"

Jane nodded. "Mr. Darcy, Aunt Gardiner, your brother, and myself. Aunt Gardiner and I were insistent that whoever was chosen would be the sort of gentleman who we ourselves would find pleasing. It was very fortuitous that Miss Darcy suggested him."

Caroline blinked. "Miss Darcy, too?"

"Yes. We all care about your happiness." Jane

pulled her lip between her teeth. "As well as our own," she added.

"I was so dreadful as to have a whole battalion against me?" Caroline shook her head. "I suppose I was," she admitted. "I did try to compromise my brother to see him married where I wished. The dining room," she said to Mrs. Nicholls. "It is the second most important room when entertaining guests," she explained to Lydia as they followed behind Netherfield's housekeeper. "The drawing room is first."

"Because you have callers more often than you have dinners, is that correct?"

"Precisely. I have a feeling you will be a natural at entertaining, Miss Lydia, as long as you can learn to act with the restraint a lady must always wear."

Lydia grimaced. "Ladies are so dull," she muttered.

"No, they are not," Caroline argued. "I have been in several houses where the lady of the house was simply delightful – always seeing that her guests were comfortable and able to converse on a wide range of topics from music to art to furnishings."

"And how does one learn such topics?"

"By listening and reading. Do you paint or sew?"

"I am absolutely abysmal at painting, but my stitching is the best of all my sisters."

"It is true," Elizabeth inserted. "Lydia knows how to make even the drabbest piece of fabric bright with a few embellishments."

Caroline looked quite pleased to hear that, but her pleasure paled to the look of happiness on Lydia's face. It was not as if Lydia had never been praised for her work before. Their mother was continually going on about how accomplished Lydia was in whatever Lydia did well. However, Elizabeth thought, with a twinge of remorse, if it was not for their mother's praise, Lydia might not receive any. She knew that she, herself, had been very remiss in bestowing approval on her younger sisters. She had always been at the ready with censure but not with commendation.

"The dining room is used daily," Miss Bingley was saying. "The arrangement goes like this..." She led Lydia to the table and began to list who sat where.

"She would make a great headmistress of a finishing school," Jane whispered, guiding Elizabeth around the edge of the room.

"She does seem to know a great deal," Elizabeth admitted, a feeling of guilt pricking her again. "I did not think she knew much. I have been horribly arrogant."

"None of us are without fault," Jane replied. "I, myself, had not considered how differently Caroline must have viewed our society. We were taught to think for ourselves. Deference is a good quality, but it is not the only quality." She leaned into Elizabeth's side more. "I think we have been taught well in that regard."

"I would agree."

Mr. Harvey had entered, and Jane turned her attention to watch the gentleman set a place as it should be set.

"He is very exact, is he not?" Jane whispered.

"As he should be," Elizabeth replied with a smile. "And he shall be your butler. You are a fortunate creature."

As she was speaking, a footman appeared at the door and stood silently waiting until Mr. Harvey had completed his demonstration.

"If I may interrupt, sir," the footman said.

"Yes, Thomas, what is it?" Mr. Harvey moved toward the door.

"There is a carriage on the drive, sir."

"A carriage, you say?"

The footman nodded. "With a crest and a trunk tied on the back, sir."

"It is not Mr. Darcy?"

"No, sir, the groom who saw it did not recognize either the carriage or the coat of arms."

"Well, Mrs. Nicholls," Mr. Harvey said. "It seems we are to have guests." He bowed and left the room quickly.

"Shall I prepare a room before we know who it is?" Mrs. Nicholls asked Caroline.

"I think it is best if we wait and see what sort of accommodation is needed. A coat of arms requires a great deal of respect, you see," she added to Lydia.

"Very well, ma'am. I will wait to hear from Harvey and select according to his information."

"That would be excellent. I am certain you will choose best. You always do." Caroline gave the housekeeper a warm smile before turning back to Lydia. "And we should make our way to the drawing room to receive our caller. Please see that my brother is made aware of his guest." And with that additional directive for Mrs. Nicholls, Caroline led

Jane, Elizabeth, and Lydia back to the drawing room.

They were just taking their places when the front door opened, and it was not long after that until a gentleman in fine clothing was standing behind Harvey at the entrance to the drawing room.

"Viscount Westonbury to see you, Miss Bingley," Harvey intoned.

The gentleman looked around the room, a furrow forming between his eyes. "I am looking for my brother, Colonel Fitzwill...i...am," his speech slowed as his eyes landed on Lydia. A slow smile crept across his face.

Lydia's eyes could not be wider, and Elizabeth understood why quite perfectly.

"You? You are the colonel's brother?" Lydia asked the exact question that was in Elizabeth's mind.

Lord Westonbury fumbled in his pocket. "I have a shilling," he said, holding up the coin. "Or..." he searched his pocket again, "I have a half-crown. I've been carrying both ever since our first meeting."

Lydia's mouth dropped open for a moment, but then she snapped it shut.

The gentleman looked at Caroline expectantly.

"My lord," she said with a curtsey, "may I present Miss Jane Bennet, Miss Elizabeth Bennet, and Miss Lydia Bennet."

Lord Westonbury's head snapped back toward Lydia. "You are Miss Lydia?"

Lydia lifted her chin. "I am, and it was Elizabeth who was with me when we met you, my lord."

He looked at Elizabeth. Something very like worry passed over his features. "Darcy's betrothed?"

"Yes," Lydia answered, arching a brow.

"Well, then, I suppose I should put my blunt back in my pocket. An angry, injured younger brother is one thing, but a furious Darcy is quite another."

"They are not returned yet," Miss Bingley said.

"It matters not. I shall keep my money in my pocket." Lord Westonbury's eyes roamed from Lydia's head to her feet and back. "It is a pity, though."

Chapter 14

"Welcome back, sir," Harvey greeted as Darcy entered the door later that same day. "I trust your journey was as good as can be expected."

"It is good to be out of the carriage," Darcy admitted. It had been a long journey.

He and Richard had stopped at an inn for one night so that Richard would be able to have a good rest. His cousin had required the assistance of some medication to sleep, however, and had been nearly as reluctant to enter the carriage this morning as he had been at Pemberley the night before they had left there.

"The colonel will need some assistance."

"Of course," Harvey waved to a footman. "Viscount Westonbury has arrived, sir," he said to Darcy while he waited for the footman to reach him. "Not more than a half hour ago."

"I will inform the colonel," Darcy said, interrupting Harvey's instructions to the footman.

"The Miss Bennets are also here, sir," Harvey added.

As he walked back to his coach, Darcy wondered if perhaps he should tell his coachman to drive on for a distance so that Richard could enter the house without so many in attendance. He was just opening the door to the carriage when a furry bundle attacked him.

"Dash! You really do need to learn how to greet a person calmly," Darcy scolded as he bent to scratch the dog's ear. "I have brought the colonel back to you, but you mustn't jump on him."

Dash cocked his head as if he understood and sat patiently at Darcy's feet while the carriage door was opened. Then, he stood with his tail wagging before returning to sitting when Darcy looked at him.

"Richard, there is someone here to greet you."

Dash barked.

"Dash?"

Darcy nodded. "He is sitting just as he should."

"Well, will you look at that. And without a biscuit on his nose," Richard said as he peeked out of the carriage door.

"Your brother is also here."

"Westonbury?"

"That is what I was told."

"Why is he here?"

"I was not informed of his reason, but I would assume that it is to see you. I did write to your parents about your injury."

Richard sighed. "And they sent him?"

"That is how it appears." Darcy paused. "He is not the only one here who might wish to see you."

Richard shook his head.

"You will have to see her eventually," Darcy spoke softly.

"Please," Richard begged as he shook his head again. "I am not ready to see her."

"Ah, here is our help." Darcy ignored his cousin's plea. There was very little that could be done to avoid Richard's having to see people.

"I do not need assistance."

Darcy leveled a glare at him. "Just as you did not need help last evening and nearly fell from the carriage to the ground?"

"Yes."

"Do try to be reasonable," Darcy chided. "I am not about to allow you to fall and risk further injury or see one of your wounds torn open. You will accept the help and do so politely."

"I am not a child. You do not need to scold me."

"I do if you are going to refuse assistance," Darcy retorted.

Dash barked.

"See. Even Dash agrees." Darcy added with a smile.

"He is just eager to see me. He is not agreeing with you."

"Then, you should be quick before he gives up his patience and leaps into the carriage."

Richard huffed and moved toward the door. He paused and closed his eyes while resting his right hand on the doorframe. He was steadying himself, and Darcy held up a hand to keep the footmen from approaching until Richard once again opened his eyes.

"I can walk to the house on my own."

"Of course, you can," Darcy agreed. "But I will be at your side if the world should decide to tip and these men will not be far behind. You will, of course, accept assistance on the steps."

"Of course," Richard muttered. He placed a hand on Darcy's arm and leaned down to scratch Dash's ear.

Darcy chuckled. "If he wags that tail any harder, it shall fly off."

Richard joined Darcy in chuckling and began his slow walk to the house.

"The drive should be much closer to the door," Richard grumbled as he mounted the steps while leaning on one of the footmen.

"I will speak to Bingley about that," Darcy teased, earning a huff from his cousin.

"It is good to see you," Bingley greeted as Richard entered the house, "even if it does look like someone got the best of you. Your room is ready and waiting." He took the place of the footman at Richard's side.

"The drawing room is rather full this afternoon," Bingley continued as they climbed the stairs. "However, no one is going to exit that room until you are settled."

"That is thoughtful of you," Richard said. "I confess to not wishing to see anyone at present."

"It was not my doing," Bingley replied.

"It was not?" Richard asked in surprise.

"Was it Caroline?" Darcy asked.

"No, it was not. Nor was it Miss Bennet or Miss Elizabeth or Georgiana or even Sir Matthew," Bingley answered.

"My brother?"

Bingley chuckled. "No, he was eager to lend you assistance, but Miss Lydia would not allow it."

"Miss Lydia?"

"Yes," Bingley said as they reached the landing and began to make their way to Richard's room. "Your brother rose to leave the room, but she stopped him."

"How did she do that?" Darcy asked. Westonbury was not the sort of gentleman to be easily put off when he wanted something.

Bingley chuckled. "She told him that she would not wish to be gawked at when ill, and she was certain the same was true for anyone."

"And my brother accepted that?"

"Not at first, but after a few moments of attempting to stare her down and dissuade her from her point of view, he conceded that it might be true that one would not necessarily even want a brother or sister gawking at them when he was ill – at least, not until the ill person was properly comfortable in bed."

Richard chuckled. "Did she bat her eyelashes at him?"

"More than once," Bingley replied.

"And did she assure him that there would be some sort of reward for doing as she suggested?" Richard asked.

Bingley's brow furrowed. "I am uncertain, although she did claim that you would likely be more welcoming if he waited. And then he asked her if he could leave the room for a shilling, which I am not sure why he would do such a thing, and she replied not even for a half-crown."

Richard stopped just inside the door to his room and turned toward Bingley. "You may tell him that for a half-crown he can see me before I am properly ensconced in bed."

Again, Bingley's brow furrowed.

"He will understand it," Richard assured Bingley.

"Were Elizabeth and her sisters visiting Caroline?" Darcy asked as Richard took a seat on the bed and allowed his man to begin the work of getting him ready to rest.

Bingley nodded. "It seems your aunt's comment about Miss Lydia's not being good enough struck a cord, and Mr. Bennet has arranged for Caroline and Georgiana to assist her in learning what she feels she must learn to be acceptable to you," he looked at Richard, "and your family."

"She thinks she is not good enough for me?" Richard grimaced as he raised his left arm to allow his shirt to be removed.

"Good heavens!" Bingley cried when he saw the gash on the side of Richard's abdomen. "You are being held together with a great number of stitches, are you not?"

"There is another on his leg," Darcy said. "We are fortunate to still have him."

"I cannot disagree," Bingley said.

"Miss Lydia thinks she is not good enough for me?" Richard repeated as his nightshirt slid over his head and covered his torso.

"Yes," Bingley answered. "Miss Elizabeth has told Jane, who told me, that Miss Lydia greatly desires your approval."

Richard said nothing in reply, though to Darcy it appeared as if his cousin was pondering that thought.

"Do you still wish to see your brother? Bingley asked as Richard was settling himself in bed.

"Yes," Richard said before sighing with relief as he lay back against his pillows. "Tell him to bring his half-crown," Richard called after Bingley. "The scoundrel," he muttered. "He best not be trying to buy any more kisses from Lydia."

"Does that mean you are not giving her up?" Darcy pulled a chair near the bed.

"No. It means she does not need to be put upon by him."

"Then you are giving her up?"

"No. I am neither giving her up or expecting her to remain attached to me. I have decided to give her the choice." He closed his eyes.

"Is the room spinning?" Darcy asked.

"As is the rest of my life," Richard replied.

"Everything will right itself eventually." Or so Darcy hoped.

"If you, and not Lydia, were to choose, what would be your choice?" Darcy prodded. He needed to know the state of his cousin's heart if he were to give Richard proper assistance. He would not push his cousin to pursue a lady who did not hold his heart any more than he would allow his cousin to hide from his heart. Darcy was nearly certain that Richard had lost his heart to Miss Lydia, and from experience, he knew that trying to deny one's heart was a torturous thing.

"I would choose to reverse time and still be in London," Richard said.

"Then, you still love her?"

Richard nodded but remained silent which was just as well since his brother had arrived at his door.

Lord Westonbury approached the bed. "You look dreadful."

"It is a pleasure to see you as well, although you will need to be on the side of the bed where Darcy is if you wish for me to actually see you."

"What do you mean?" Westonbury moved to the far side of the bed.

"The blow to his head has damaged his eyesight. We do not know if it is a lasting thing or just temporary like the spinning room and unsteadiness when he walks."

"You cannot see out of your left eye?"

"No, I can see out of it as long as everything is in front of me. I just cannot see anything that is to that side of me."

"That is very odd," Westonbury propped himself on the edge of the bed, and Richard held out his hand.

"Your half-crown." Richard's tone was flat as he held his brother's gaze.

"I am not giving you my half-crown."

"You are also not going to offer it to Miss Lydia for any reason," Richard replied.

Westonbury chuckled. "You heard about Sally's did you?"

"We found Miss Lydia and Miss Elizabeth there if that is what you mean," Darcy said.

"What do you mean found?"

"Come now, Wes," Richard said, "you do not truly believe that either Miss Bennet was at Sally's for an appointment, now do you?"

Westonbury shrugged. "I suppose I had not considered why they were there. I only just found out that the pretty young thing that swindled me out of a shilling and gave me a sore nose was the lady with whom I heard you are enamoured." He shifted on the bed. "Why were they there?"

"How did you learn about Miss Lydia?" Richard asked.

Westonbury shook his head. "No, I asked you

a question first — but we could wrestle for to see who answers first. However, I do believe I would win this time."

There was only a year separating Richard and his brother, so wrestling to settle a disagreement was not an unusual thing for the two of them. They had broken more than one vase while attempting to settle a dispute in such a fashion. Richard was an inch shorter than his brother, though he was just as broad. However, shorter did not mean easily overcome, for most often, Richard had been victorious.

"You could wrestle Darcy," Richard offered.

"No, he cannot," Darcy replied. "He cheats."

Westonbury grinned. "So does Richard."

"Which is why you both usually beat me," Darcy replied. "So, let's consider me beaten in Richard's stead, which means Richard will answer your question before you tell us that Aunt Catherine told you about Miss Lydia."

"Aunt Catherine knows about Miss Lydia?"

Darcy nodded. "She was here in an attempt to talk me out of marrying Elizabeth and into marrying Anne instead."

"I knew she had gone to hunt you down," Westonbury said with a smirk, "but I heard nothing of Miss Lydia."

"Well, then, I recant. You were soundly beaten by me in our imagined wrestling match, and so you must explain how you know about Miss Lydia." Darcy had been confident that if Westonbury knew about Lydia that Lady Catherine had returned to town and told one and all at Matlock House about her.

"No, I beat you. Now, brother dear, kindly explain to me why you were looking for your lady at Sally's."

Richard drew and released a breath. "Wickham," he snarled.

"And how did you find out about Miss Lydia?" Darcy asked.

"But there is a story behind Richard's answer," Westonbury protested.

"After you give us the name of your source, we can share stories."

"You could wrestle him, and, if you win, you get your story first, but, if he wins, you tell us the name of the gossip who told you about Miss Lydia," Richard offered.

"I am still not wrestling," Darcy said. "How is it

that you are both older than me and still act like you are far younger?"

Westonbury shrugged. "Because we are not you."

Darcy rolled his eyes.

"Very well," Westonbury said. "I heard about her from Mrs. Salter."

Chapter 15

"Mrs. Salter?" Darcy repeated.

He had not thought to hear that name again, especially not from one of his relations. He had not even considered that Mrs. Salter might be a name any of his relatives would know. But then, if anyone were to know her, it would be Westonbury as he made it his business to know of as many as possible of the ladies who would be parading their charges through the season. Much could be deciphered about a daughter by knowing the mother — or so his cousin claimed.

Westonbury nodded. "Do you know her?"

"I know of her."

"You do?" Richard asked in surprise. "I cannot say I have heard the name before."

Richard, unlike his brother, only felt he needed to know those mothers who had daughters that piqued his interest. Of course, he was also more likely to sequester himself away in a library or card room to talk to the fathers and brothers than his elder brother was.

"Do you remember how I told you that Miss Bingley did not seem so bad after hearing Mr. Bennet's tale about Mrs. Bennet?" Darcy asked.

Richard shook his head slowly.

"It was the night after the ladies had come back from shopping and you were asked to choose the best red ribbon."

Westonbury laughed. "You were picking ribbons?"

"Miss Lydia needed an opinion," Darcy said.

That information did little to keep Richard's brother from chuckling further.

"She values his opinion on many things." Darcy held Richard's gaze.

"Yes, I remember that conversation." Richard's reply was quick and lacking in any emotion. However, his gaze dropped away from Darcy's.

"It was just before Miss Lydia and her sister went missing," Darcy explained to Westonbury with the hope of bringing to Richard's mind the fear they had both felt that night when they had thought their ladies were in danger.

"Yes, I know," Richard snapped. "Continue. How does that apply to this Mrs. Salter?"

"She was the lady in Mr. Bennet's story who treated Mrs. Bennet very ill."

Richard's eyes grew wide. "And you say, Wes, that she told you about Miss Lydia?"

"She did not tell me directly," Westonbury replied, rising to cross to the window. "I overheard her talking to a friend at Almack's. It seems her daughter was on the point of being happily betrothed until the fellow found someone else – with deeper pockets and a more willing charm – that is how she said it. Just like that, with a suggestive lilt to her tone. She then added that Miss –" He waved his hand in a circle in front of him as if attempting to draw a scent towards himself.

The action was familiar to Darcy. His cousin had always made that same motion when attempting to recall something.

"Oh, I cannot remember! But it matters not who she is to me. However, according to Mrs. Salter, the girl had no choice but to accept this fellow's proposal. Her willing charms had found her in a desperate state you see." He lifted a brow.

"With child?" Richard asked.

His brother nodded from where he leaned against the wall near the window. "It seems that Mrs. Salter had experienced somewhat of the same treatment when she was young. Some willing wench – I swear she used those words – stole her prize from her. And she had seen this woman in town with Miss Darcy – of all people!" He said the last part in a womanly falsetto.

"Well, that caught my attention, so I stayed where I was, twirling my quizzing glass and pretending to watch the dancing."

"She was speaking poorly of my sister?" Darcy asked. How dare the woman do such a thing!

"Not directly, but it was implied."

"She's either stupid or has no clue who Darcy is," Richard grumbled.

"My money is on stupid." Westonbury pushed off the wall. "To get to the point. After a discussion of who Darcy was and his connections – meaning our father – Mrs. Salter then said that the woman's daughters seemed to be cut from the same cloth. There was something about a compromise at a ball involving one of them, and a discussion of two others grasping far above their station. Apparently, she had heard that the youngest was vying for the affections of the Earl of Matlock's youngest son. Someone had seen them walking together or some such thing. No names were given. I had to discover the name of the youngest Bennet on my own, which was not easily or cheaply done. The servants at Almack's expect remuneration for being nosy."

"You did not just ask her?" Richard scoffed.

"She had not seen me and after speaking of Miss Lydia – whose name I did not know at that time – she then suggested to her friend that she thought her daughter might be able to do one better and snare me. Trust me, if you have ever met Miss Salter, you will understand why I was in a desperate state to be gone and not discovered by Mrs. Salter."

"Is she not handsome?" Darcy asked.

"Her features are very pleasant – her spirit is not. If I am to be tied to a wife, it shall not be a lady of her ilk." He shuddered. "And since I have no intention of being trapped by anyone, when Mrs. Salter's friend teased that Miss Salter could affect a compromise and Mrs. Salter congratulated her on a delightful plan, I found the door quickly – after enlisting a servant to discover the information I sought and having him deliver it to me in my carriage."

"That will not make it any easier for Miss Lydia to establish herself in town," Darcy muttered.

"Which is another good reason for her to give me up," Richard replied.

"Wait! If you have not formed an attachment to her, why can I not give her a half-crown for a kiss or two?" Westonbury asked. "She is a pretty thing."

Darcy folded his arm and looked at Richard, waiting to see how his cousin would explain himself.

"She is a gentleman's daughter, not some trollop," Richard argued. "You do not go around paying gentlemen's daughters for favours."

"You and Darcy might not," Westonbury teased. "Clarice was a gentleman's daughter, but she found herself in need of employment."

"Clarice? I assume you are speaking of one of the women at Sally's," Richard said.

If Richard could have gotten out of bed or even moved enough to reach his brother, who had returned to sit on the end of the bed, it looked to Darcy from the expression Richard wore and the tone he used, that Westonbury would not win such an altercation.

"I am."

"Miss Lydia is not one of Sally's women," Richard growled.

"Nor is she your lady," Westonbury argued.

"She is..." Richard snapped his mouth closed on his bellow, seeming to shrink further into his pillow as he did so.

"She is if she wishes to be," Darcy finished Richard's thought.

"What do you mean?" Westonbury asked the question of Darcy, but his eyes slid to his brother, who had his eyes closed.

"Look at me," Richard said. "Why should anyone be tied to this?"

"I still do not follow. You have never been particularly handsome."

Darcy gaped at his cousin. Did the man not think before he spoke?

"Your appeal has always been in your charm and caring nature," Westonbury said.

He did think before he spoke. Darcy's lips tipped up in pleased surprise.

"But I will likely lose my commission," Richard argued.

"And mother will be happy for it."

Richard's eyes opened. "I will need an income."

"Father will see to that."

"Not if they do not approve of my choice of bride."

Westonbury clapped his hands. "So you do like her, do you?"

"Of course, I do," Richard snapped.

"Well, she seems enamoured with you as well. There is a good deal of gumption in her. She did swindle me out of my money and gave me a sore nose in the process."

"Not to mention," said Darcy, "that she prevented Wes from seeing you before you sent for him. How many people keep him from what he wants?"

"Exactly!" Westonbury agreed. "And I am not entirely sure how she managed it. I was determined to outwit her."

"She batted her eyes," Richard said.

Westonbury's brow furrowed. "She did, but I am not unaccustomed to that."

"She is a Bennet," Darcy said. "They do seem to possess a power that few others do."

Westonbury laughed. "That is the most ridiculous thing I think I have ever heard you say, Darcy."

"It may sound ridiculous, but I assure you it is true. I helped stage the compromise of which Mrs. Salter was speaking."

The sound of a maid passing the door was the only sound that penetrated the room for a full two minutes while Westonbury stared, open-mouthed at Darcy.

"It was necessary to be able to give me a chance of winning Elizabeth's heart," Darcy said as he pushed up from his chair. "Speaking of whom, I should like to see her before she goes home." He looked at Richard. "Do you wish to see Lydia?"

His cousin smiled sadly. "With all my heart, but I cannot."

"Then, I shall pass along your sorrow at needing to rest instead of seeing her," Westonbury said as he joined Darcy in standing.

"No, Darcy can do that."

Westonbury shook his head. "Darcy has his own lady who will claim his attention."

"You are a –"

"Yes, I am," Westonbury cut his brother's words off. "Get some rest," he added before turning to leave. "Richard," he called from the door.

"Yes."

"I am pleased you were not injured any further than you were."

"I wish I could say I am as well," Richard replied, "However, I have not yet decided if I am pleased or not."

~*~*~

"He is in a sorry state, is he not?" Westonbury said to Darcy when they were both in the hall.

"He wanted to stay at Pemberley."

"Because of Miss Lydia?"

Darcy nodded.

Westonbury blew out a breath as he stood at the top of the stairs. "I am uncertain how Mother will take the news of her son marrying someone with no standing in her circles." He cast a look back toward Richard's room. "However, he is excessively smitten."

The two cousins began their descent of the stairs.

"Go to the library," Westonbury said when they

were about halfway down. "I will have Miss Elizabeth meet you there."

Darcy eyed his cousin suspiciously.

Catching Darcy's eye, Westonbury smiled. "I shall require a detailed account of the compromise you were part of in return for my service." He clapped Darcy on the shoulder as they gained the landing. "A gentleman who has been separated from the lady he fancies should not have to be reunited with her where there is an audience."

Darcy chuckled. "I see your point, but there is Lydia."

"Trust me. If she were any other man's lady, I might attempt to charm her away from him, but not my brother – or you, but she is not your lady," he added quickly.

"She is my sister – or will be," Darcy cautioned.

"And I will treat her as I do Georgiana. Now, go."

Darcy thanked him and hurried to the library. There was still a niggling fear that he should have been the one to speak to Lydia about Richard, but Westonbury had always been gentle with Georgiana. Surely, Darcy could trust him with this. Besides, he would be able to see Lydia before she left.

He made a circuit of the library while he waited for Elizabeth. Bingley did need to work on acquiring a few more books. The shelves were not barren, but they were not as full as Darcy thought they should be.

"Fitzwilliam?"

Darcy sighed in relief. She was here. He turned toward her and opened his arms, and she wasted no time in finding her way into his embrace.

"I have missed you," he said as he held her close.

"And I have missed you." She squeezed him more tightly.

"Kiss me."

She lifted her head from where it rested on his heart and tipped her face up towards him.

He cradled the back of her head with his hand and lowered his lips to hers, kissing her gently, longingly.

"When can we marry?" he asked.

"Tomorrow?" she replied.

He chuckled. "That is likely too soon, I suppose. Your mother would not be best pleased to be rushed in planning a wedding breakfast. And Richard would not be able to attend. Nor could I leave him here without me."

She cupped his cheek. "If his recovery is to be of a long duration, I can join you here. I do not care where we are as long as we are together."

He dipped his head and kissed her once again. He was of the same mind. He wished to never be parted from her again, but that time was not yet. "When Richard is able to join us for the wedding breakfast, then we shall marry."

"And if he refuses to attend?"

Darcy sighed. "I am trusting that he will recover in mind as quickly as he does in body."

"A week will tell us more," Elizabeth assured him. "It is all very new."

"How is Lydia?"

"She is shaken and fearful. It is very unlike her."

Darcy's heart broke at the revelation.

"However," Elizabeth continued, "I will be very surprised if she does not rise to the challenge. A Bennet always does. Look at what Jane did to claim her love."

How fortunate was he to have a lady who could tease him into better spirits even in the face of such uncertainty?

"And if she does not?"

"I shall love you, and we shall face it together."

"That is a very good plan," Darcy said, pulling away from her some to smile down at her. "Now, before my cousin formulates some scandalous story about why you were absent for so long, we should return you to the drawing room."

"Should I worry about him?" Elizabeth asked as she wrapped her arm around Darcy's.

"Not overly much," Darcy assured her. "Wes and Richard are not just brothers but good friends. He is a scoundrel, but he knows his place. He will behave as he should." Darcy leaned his head towards her ear. "He also knows that neither Richard or I would allow him to treat poorly anyone for whom we cared. And I care very dearly for you, Miss Elizabeth Bennet."

"And I, you, Mr. Darcy." They had stopped outside the drawing room and, lifting onto her toes, she kissed his cheek before the door was opened and they left their private moment behind.

Chapter 16

"Good day, my lord. How does your brother fare today?" Elizabeth asked when Darcy, Bingley, and Lord Westonbury entered the sitting room at Longbourn.

"Well enough to order me out of his room," Westonbury replied with a grin.

"He was resting when we left," Darcy added, glancing around the room.

"Our mother was needed in the kitchen," Jane said.

"Ah, I was wondering where she was."

"Was it too quiet a greeting?" Elizabeth teased.

Darcy chuckled. "In a word? Yes."

"Then, Mr. Darcy, you will be delighted to know that she is anxiously awaiting her opportunity to meet a real lord, so your desire for an effusive greeting will not go unmet," Elizabeth said. "And then, we shall go for a walk."

"Where our mother's delights will no longer be able to be heard," Mary muttered from where she sat in the corner of the room.

Elizabeth gave Mary a stern look. It was one thing to add sardonic comments to a conversation when it was just their close family and friends who were present. It was another thing altogether when one was entertaining a person of importance whose opinion could affect the future happiness of a lady's sisters. As was normal, a stern glare did little to affect Mary, who merely stared blankly in return as if to say, "but it is true." And it was true. Elizabeth knew that her mother would not greet Lord Westonbury quietly, for the more excited their mother became, the louder her voice grew.

"Lord Westonbury, this is my sister Mary," Jane said, "and next to Lydia is Kitty. Mary, Kitty, this is Mr. Darcy's cousin, the Viscount Westonbury."

Mary placed her sewing aside and rose – reluctantly, it seemed to Elizabeth – to curtsey and greet Lord Westonbury properly.

"And tell me, Miss Mary," Westonbury said,

making his way across the room to sit near her, "should I fear this introduction to your mother?"

Mary raised an eyebrow at him. "You are likely safe as long as you do not tell her that you know Sally." She leaned around him to see Lydia. "That was the lady's name at the brothel, was it not?"

"Mary!" Elizabeth scolded. "A proper lady does not speak of such things."

"And an honourable gentleman does not do such things, and yet here we are." She gave Westonbury an appraising look but said no more.

"I am not offended," Westonbury said.

Mary opened her mouth to speak but closed it again when Elizabeth glared at her. "Then, allow me to be offended on your behalf. I assure you that my sisters do know how to comport themselves properly."

Again, Mary's brow rose as if to ask, "do we?"

Darcy took Elizabeth's hand in his, drawing her attention away from her troublesome sister. Mary was far too opinionated and outspoken at times. How anyone as wonderful as Mr. Darcy wished to tie himself to a family such as hers at this moment beyond her! However, Elizabeth was exceptionally glad for his willingness.

"I have written to my aunt and uncle, informing them that Richard is well and has been installed in a room at Netherfield," Darcy said.

"Will they visit him?" Lydia asked.

"I would expect that, at least, my mother would visit, but I am sure my father will join her if he has no pressing matters which must come first," Westonbury said.

"And will he see them?" Lydia had been very sorry to not have been allowed to see with her own eyes that the colonel was not in grave danger.

"I imagine he will not be given the choice," Westonbury replied. "My mother is not the sort of lady to be put off."

"Is she pleasant?" Lydia was twisting her fingers in her lap, an action that seemed not to go unnoticed by Westonbury.

"She is, though she can also be demanding." He smiled. "However, I am certain she will be happy to meet all of Richard's new friends and relations."

It appeared as if Lydia wished to inquire further, but just at that moment, Mrs. Bennet entered the room, and Mr. Darcy rose first to greet her and then introduce her to his cousin, effectively putting an end to any previous conversation.

"A real lord – in my home!" Mrs. Bennet was overflowing with delight. "There will not be a neighbour who will not be jealous of my good fortune, I must say." She paused. "However, it would be a much more delightful thing to be called on by someone such as yourself, my lord, if the honour did not come because of the injury to our dear colonel."

"I would agree. An injury is not something someone ever wishes on those they hold dear," Westonbury said.

"My husband will be sorry to have missed your visit, my lord, but he is gone out to view a tenant's home today." She turned to Mr. Darcy. "Sir William was kind enough to take him in his cart, and I was able to send a few things for the tenant's wife in the back of it. It was really just the thing, but then Sir William is often thinking about practicalities such as that."

"Sir William is a delight!" Bingley said.

"Indeed, he is!" Mrs. Bennet agreed. "Mr. Bennet and Sir William have been particular friends for years." She smiled softly. "He never once questioned my becoming mistress of Longbourn. His wife..." She did not finish the thought. "Lady Lucas and I have become dear friends, of course. It was only natural that it should happen, you see, as our husbands spend so much time in one another's company."

"You were not friends with Lady Lucas before you married Papa?" Lydia asked.

"Oh, we knew one another, but we were no more than acquaintances."

"How very odd," Lydia said. "I had thought you were always friends."

"That is because we are such good friends now," Mrs. Bennet replied. "And it was a very little trial to become better acquainted once I was married to your father. One just presents herself as who she is even if she does not feel completely up to the challenge and eventually, one finally believes it herself." She turned to Lord Westonbury. "Would you care for tea now or after you have toured the area? Lizzy tells me that you are all to walk out. I had thought after, but I was not certain if that would be acceptable to you."

"I am amenable to after," Westonbury said.

"That is very gracious of you, my lord." She beamed at him. "I will not keep you from your walk, then, but will wait to hear about your family when you return." Her brow furrowed. "Is there a Lady Westonbury?"

"Not yet."

Her brows rose. "But there is one who will soon be?"

"No, I fear, there is not."

"Oh, that is unfortunate," Mrs. Bennet said with some feeling. "A handsome gentleman such as yourself should not be unattached."

Mary mumbled something that, to Elizabeth, sounded a lot like, "Yes, he should be."

"I apologize, Miss Mary. I did not quite catch that," Westonbury said, leaning his head closer to her.

"There was nothing to be caught," she replied, though her cheeks did grow faintly red.

"Shall we be off then?" Bingley stood quickly, much more quickly than Elizabeth had ever seen him do before. Perhaps he too feared what might come out of Mary's mouth next if they were not to leave the room quickly.

Bonnets and wraps were at the ready, so the preparation for departure was very little, and they were off quickly.

Mrs. Bennet saw them to the door herself, or

more accurately, she saw Lord Westonbury to the door and made certain to tell him at least twice more how delighted she was to have met him.

"That was not so very bad," Westonbury said when they were well away from the house.

"Indeed, it was not," Mary agreed.

Westonbury stopped dead in his tracks. "Was Miss Mary just agreeable?"

"I believe she was," Lydia replied when no one else said anything.

"I try to always agree with that which is correct," Mary retorted.

"Ah, I see." Westonbury smirked at her, causing her to scowl.

"Mary, will you walk with me," Elizabeth said. It was probably best for Mary to be separated from the viscount.

"I am going to walk with Kitty," Mary answered.

"I am walking with Lydia," Kitty replied.

"My arm is not taken," Westonbury offered.

Mary looked at the arm he offered, raised a brow while giving him a look of perturbed displeasure, and then very cautiously placed her hand on it.

"Why?" Bingley whispered to Darcy as the group began walking once again. "She obviously does not like him. Why would he subject himself to what could very likely be a lecture?"

"I was thinking the same thing," Elizabeth admitted. "It is as if he wishes to provoke her."

Darcy sighed. "I cannot answer with any certainty, but I do not think he has ever met someone who is so completely unaffected by either his title or charm – at least, not a female someone."

"He will not sway her opinion," Jane said. "Once Mary's good opinion is gone, it is excessively hard to reclaim."

"It would take an act of heroic proportions," Elizabeth agreed.

Mary was firm in her resolve. That was why Mary wore dresses without a lot of adornment. She did not like flounces and ribbons, and no amount of protest or persuasion by their mother or younger sisters had ever convinced Mary that she should do more than add a row of flowers around a hem or neckline. Simply put, Mary was not overly ornate. She was as she dressed – practical, sturdy, and modest nearly to the point of being dull.

"Mary!" Lydia snapped, drawing the attention of one and all.

"I assure you that I am not offended overly much," Westonbury said.

Elizabeth's breath caught. What had Mary said while she had not been paying attention?

"A great deal of our argument was my doing." Westonbury looked at Darcy sheepishly. "I overstepped."

"You are not the only one, then!" Lydia cried. "Mary has no business speaking as she did to anyone let alone Colonel Fitzwilliam's brother. Why just think how he would feel to hear you attacking his brother!"

"I was not attacking him," Mary protested. "I was making a point – a very good and extremely accurate point!"

Lydia stamped her foot. "It was not proper. Do you wish for him to think we are not proper? Do you truly want him to tell his parents and his brother that we are not fit to be known to them?"

"I would never –"

"You might if she continues down the path she has chosen." Lydia folded her arms and scowled at Mary.

Westonbury looked to Darcy in confusion.

Elizabeth sighed and, with a sad smile for Darcy, she dropped his arm and went to Mary.

"I think it might be best if we were to walk together."

"But what of Mr. Darcy," Mary said.

"Mr. Darcy is not causing a scene," Elizabeth replied.

"And neither am I. Lydia is doing that."

"Because you were being rude!"

"I was not being rude. I was being honest."

"The two are not always exclusive," Jane said. "Sometimes honest facts can be presented in a very unpolite fashion."

"And they were!" Lydia said.

Mary's eyes narrowed. "I would have rather stayed at home and read anyway. I only came because Lydia wanted it." She lifted her chin and began stalking silently homeward.

"We do not wish for you to leave," Westonbury called after her.

"It may not be what you wish," she retorted, "but it is what you have gotten."

"She is impossible," Lydia said with another stamp of her foot.

"Shall I go after her?" Jane asked.

Elizabeth shook her head. When Mary was in high dudgeon, there was little anyone could say to help her see reason. Later, after there had been time enough for her to calm, then she could be more easily approached.

"I could go after her," Westonbury offered. "It was my fault. I did provoke her." Again, he cast a sheepishly apologetic look at Darcy before turning to Lydia. "I must apologize for causing your unease, Miss Lydia. It was not done intentionally." He pulled a handkerchief from his pocket. "Will you forgive me so that Darcy will stop scowling at me?"

Lydia took the handkerchief from him and began dabbing at her eyes while she glanced back at Darcy, who was indeed scowling at his cousin. She nodded her head. "I should hate to see your face bruised on my account."

"You think he would hit me?"

Again, Lydia nodded. "I did not think he knew how either," she whispered. "However, I have seen Mr. Wickham and can assure you that Mr. Darcy can hit very effectively."

"Is that so?" Westonbury said as he took Lydia's

hand and tucked it in the crook of his elbow before extending his other arm to Kitty. "Do tell."

Elizabeth shrugged as she met Darcy's gaze. "My sisters sometimes argue."

"As do mine," Bingley said. "Think nothing of it. It shall all get sorted out in time. It always does."

Elizabeth blew out a breath. "But the sorting out can be arduous," she said to Darcy who had reached where she stood.

Darcy took Elizabeth's hand and prevented her from walking on with Jane and Bingley. "I will speak to my troublesome cousin," he assured her before lifting her hand to his lips and kissing it. "Hopefully, he will be easily sorted."

Chapter 17

Mary huffed as she stood beside Elizabeth, waiting to be allowed entrance to Netherfield the next day. There had been a long and lengthy discussion between Mary and her father after Lydia had told him what Mary had said on their walk.

"You are to be polite," Lydia said.

"I know," Mary grumbled.

"And apologize."

Again, Mary huffed. "I know. Stop speaking."

"Good day, Mr. Harvey," Jane said as the door opened. "We are here to see..." She looked at her sisters. "Well, everyone it seems."

"Very good, ma'am. If you will follow me."

"That lace Mama selected looked very nice on Elizabeth's wedding dress, did it not?" Jane asked Lydia. She was attempting as always to direct the conversation so that the argument from a few moments ago would be lost.

"It was lovely," Lydia agreed.

"Only two more weeks," Kitty whispered, "and we shall have to call on you here, Jane."

Jane smiled broadly. "It seems so far away and yet so close."

When he had asked, their mother had assured Darcy yesterday that she thought all the necessary preparations for a wedding would be completed by the end of the week. There was nothing to be concerned about except whether Colonel Fitzwilliam would be able to attend and if standing for a full service would be too much for Mr. Bennet's leg. Therefore, a date had finally been decided upon, and Elizabeth knew that Jane was eagerly anticipating becoming the mistress of Netherfield.

Dash was the first to greet the Bennet ladies when they entered the drawing room, but after a proper greeting, which consisted of a scratched ear, he sat down next to Lydia. Kitty and Georgiana excused themselves to go to the music room. Mary attempted to join them, but Jane, who was rarely stern, grasped her hand firmly.

"You have something you must do first," Jane whispered.

Mary blew out a breath and with flushed cheeks turned to Lord Westonbury. "My lord," she said and waited for him to acknowledge her, "I have come today with a very particular purpose. I have been made aware of the fact that though what I said to you yesterday was entirely truthful, it was not my place to say it even if no one else seems to wish to speak on the behalf of the less fortunate –"

Jane cleared her throat.

"What I am attempting to say," Mary corrected, "is that my words were out of place and so I would ask your forgiveness for my immoderate behaviour."

"My forgiveness is readily given. However, I must also apologize for provoking you to behave so." He held out his hand to her. "Am I forgiven?"

"For provoking me."

"Nothing else?" Westonbury's lips curled into a smirk, and Darcy coughed. "Yes, well, that is all for which I have asked forgiveness, is it not?" His hand remained outstretched to her.

Mary looked at his hand. Then, with a raised

brow and a look that did not speak of a willingness to bestow forgiveness, she placed her hand in his.

He gave it a firm shake and then, lifted it to lips.

Mary gasped and snatched her hand away. "That is not necessary."

"I think it is."

"It is my hand, and I think it is not. Therefore, it is not."

"But it is what is polite," Westonbury protested.

"I am not to argue with you, my lord," Mary replied.

"A pity that," Westonbury muttered.

"Tea!" Bingley inserted. "I think it would be very good to have tea, do you not, Darcy?"

"An excellent idea," Darcy agreed.

"And Miss Lydia, you may help me pour," Caroline said happily.

"Wes," Darcy called to his cousin, who was still standing with Mary and offering to see her to the music room, "I believe she knows the way."

"It seems we are to be kept apart," Westonbury said with a laugh.

"It is for the best," Mary assured him.

"I am not entirely certain I agree."

"Of course, you would not. It is a logical and well-thought-out plan."

"I am not incapable of logical thinking."

Mary raised a brow and shook her head. "You have yet to prove it, my lord." Then, she curtseyed and left the room.

Westonbury flopped into a chair. "You are a dreadful bore, Darcy."

Darcy laughed. "Not everyone enjoys an argument as much as you."

"I can argue with you if you wish," Sir Matthew quipped.

Westonbury sighed. "I think I shall pass."

"I am here if you should feel the need to disagree with someone," Sir Matthew added.

Lydia followed Caroline out of the room to see that the tea service was being prepared and likely to discuss some other facet of being a proper hostess. It surprised Elizabeth how discreet Caroline was being. There was no announcement of a lesson's topic nor was there any indication that it was not the most normal thing in all the world for Caroline and Lydia to be heading off together to do something or another.

Jane took a seat next to Mr. Bingley, and the

two began discussing what preparations for their upcoming wedding were being made today while she was away from home.

"Your mother does not mind that you are leaving so much to her?" Bingley asked.

"Not at all. We will do our part when we return home. Father was much more eager that we see to Mary," Jane replied.

Westonbury shifted uneasily in his chair.

"Troubles?" Darcy asked him.

"I had not intended for her to get in trouble," Westonbury whispered. "Perhaps I should apologize for that?"

"When she returns," Darcy replied.

The conversation then fell into the realm of topics commonly canvased in a drawing room – the weather, the neighbours, and the health of those family members who were ailing, namely Mr. Bennet and Colonel Fitzwilliam.

"Do you think he will see her?" Elizabeth whispered to Darcy. Lydia had eaten little yesterday or today. Between the worry over the damage Mary might have done by being so outspoken to Lord Westonbury and concern about the colonel, she had little appetite and wandered from room to room unable to focus on any task. To be honest, Elizabeth was more than a little anxious about the state of her youngest sister's mind.

"We are hopeful," Darcy replied.

"It would be excellent if he did."

"I agree," Darcy replied. "One way or the other, a decision must be arrived at eventually." He took Elizabeth's hand in his and simply held it.

"I will take him some tea," Westonbury said as the tea service was brought in. "If I cannot argue with Miss Mary, I might as well see if I can persuade my brother to be reasonable."

"Do not go to the music room," Darcy cautioned.

Westonbury leveled a severe look at him before turning away to gather the tea for himself and Richard.

"He is..." Elizabeth sought for the right word.

"Troublesome and used to getting his way," Darcy finished.

"Do I need to worry about him?" It was the same question she had asked Darcy after meeting Lord Westonbury for the first time.

"I would like to say no," Darcy answered with a sigh, "but, to be honest, I am uncertain. I do not fear for your safety or that of your sisters. However, I do fear for everyone's sanity at this point. What Miss Mary said to him yesterday seems to have struck a chord with him."

"I was shocked to hear what she had said," Elizabeth replied. "I know she does not approve of places such as Sally's."

"Which is as it should be," Darcy inserted, and Elizabeth agreed.

"And I know that she is given to moralizing, but she has always confined her speeches to those she knows well. It is truly not like her to speak as she did to a stranger – most especially, one who is due a certain amount of respect just because of who he is. I have been attempting to deduce the reason, but I have not yet discovered it."

"Have you asked her?"

Elizabeth nodded. "Her reply was not helpful." She attended to the tea she had been served. "Lydia is doing very well."

"And Caroline looks excessively pleased," Darcy added.

This, of course, led to a discussion about Darcy's aunt and Lydia's desire to do well.

When tea was nearly over, Darcy went to inquire

of Richard whether or not he would be amenable to guests.

Elizabeth sighed with relief when he returned and gave her a smile and a nod before informing Lydia that the colonel would be delighted to have her visit him.

"Come, my love."

Happily, Elizabeth placed her hand in his and together, they went up with Lydia.

"Wait," Lydia said as Darcy reached for the doorknob. She blew out a breath. "I do not know if I can do this," she whispered.

"Do you not wish to see him?" Elizabeth asked.

"Oh, very much, but what if he is too greatly altered?"

"He does not look as he did," Darcy answered. "His injuries are still fairly recent."

She shook her head. "That is not what I meant."

"Is it not?" Elizabeth asked. "I know you were worried about that." Had they not had a discussion about whether or not Lydia could love someone who was not handsome?

"I will not lie. That is still a small fear, but..." Her eyes filled with tears and she wrapped an arm around her middle. "He did not wish to see me. What if he no longer loves me?"

Elizabeth wrapped Lydia in her arms. "He will still love you."

"How can you say so?"

"If he did not love you, he would not be so concerned about not being good enough for you," Darcy replied.

"But he is!" Lydia said with some force.

"Then, you must convince him of that," Darcy replied. "His mind and heart are muddled. His life is not what it was, and it is likely that it never will be what it was."

Lydia nodded and dashed away the few tears which had escaped her eyes.

"Not knowing is far worse than knowing," Darcy added. "I know."

"You do?"

He nodded. "I thought your sister hated me and would always hate me even though I loved her dearly. That is why I took part in the scheme to see Miss Bingley and Sir Matthew betrothed. I needed to know if I had a chance. Your sister Jane and your aunt seemed to think I did. Thankfully, they were correct."

"I am also happy they were," Lydia agreed with a smile. "You are very nice when one gets to know you. Not at all as you appeared to be when you first arrived at Netherfield."

Darcy chuckled. "Thank you, Miss Lydia. I am happy to know I improve upon acquaintance. Now, shall we take on the surly Colonel Fitzwilliam and attempt to convince him that he is not unworthy?"

Lydia nodded and pulled in a deep breath as Darcy opened the door.

"Richard," Darcy said, motioning for Lydia to follow him to the far side of the bed, "I have brought you some guests."

Lydia's hand rested on her heart and tears spilled down her cheek.

"I look dreadful."

"You do," she agreed, approaching his bed. "Does it hurt horridly?" She took his hand. "I'll not move your shoulder," she added. "I understand it is also injured."

"It is not as bad as it was," Richard replied.

"The room spins, and he can see you best when you are on this side of him," Darcy added.

"I wish I could take it away," Lydia whispered. "How dreadfully boring it must be to lie here and have nothing to do but consider if you hurt more today than yesterday." She perched on the side of the bed.

"It is rather dull except when Darcy or Westonbury are here. Did you know that each swag of the flounce around the top of the bed on this side has between four and six folds?"

Lydia peered up at the material. "You are right!" She then looked at the other side of the bed. "It is the same on the side you cannot see." She sighed and smiled at him. "I have missed you, and I was so dreadfully afraid you had died."

Darcy handed her his handkerchief and then, without a word, he and Elizabeth left the room.

"And I missed you," Richard said. He wished to pull her to him and kiss away her tears, but he knew he could not. "I would understand if you did not wish for me to continue –"

"Do not say it!" Lydia interrupted. "You shall not be rid of me that easily!"

"But I am not who I was." She needed to know who she was accepting.

"Yes, you are. In your heart, you are."

Richard grimaced as he lifted her hand to his lips. "You really will accept me as I am?"

She nodded, and Richard expelled a deep breath that carried with it many of the worries and fears which had settled upon him as soon as he had woken and found his life set on its end.

Chapter 18

Richard pushed up from the edge of his bed, where he had been waiting for the world to stop spinning. Since the room seemed to be standing still, it should now be safe to walk the short distance between the bed and the door.

Slowly, with deliberate steps, he crossed the floor but paused when he reached the door to lean his head against it for a moment to allow the room to still itself once again before opening the door.

He could not continue to stay in this room as he had for the last several days. He grew weary of seeing the same portion of ceiling and window. He wanted to attempt returning to normal, everyday life. He needed to do so, for how was he ever to be good enough for Lydia if he did not at some point get out of bed and on with his duties.

He stepped into the hallway, but then, thinking

better of it as the hall seemed to waver and he imagined making a spectacle of himself by falling down the stairs, he returned to his room but not to his bed. Instead, he turned the chair near the hearth so that it would face the open door. This way, he could, at least, catch glimpses of life while his blasted head took its sweet time healing.

With a grimace, he sat down and immediately realized that he had not moved a footstool into position for his feet. That was foolish, for he was not getting up to do it now! He would do without being able to prop up his legs until someone came into the room who would not fall over when bending to move such a piece of furniture.

"The upstairs maid sees to the cleaning of this hallway and the hearths in each of the rooms."

Richard tipped his head. Was that Caroline?

"There is another maid who sees to the hall and hearths downstairs. Of course, they will perform these duties at times when they will not be seen or will be least intrusive. One does not wish to have her private conversations carried to others."

"Would they do that?"

Was that Lydia? Richard considered getting up and going to the hall to discover what Lydia and

Caroline were doing, but his body was protesting not being in bed as it was. He dared not push it further than he already had.

"Miss Bingley," he called.

"Oh, yes, it is often the servants who spread the most damaging news in town. One can never be too careful."

"How very odd."

He smiled at Lydia's tone of wonder. "Miss Bingley," he called again.

Footsteps drew nearer. And then a face appeared in his doorway. Not just one face, but two. The one he wished most to see was just behind the one to whom he had called.

"Good day, Miss Bingley, Miss Lydia."

"Why are you out of bed?" Lydia demanded. "Has the surgeon said you may be?"

"I am tired of lying there," he replied. "And I am only sitting. It is not so great a strain as one might think." His lips curled into a smile for her.

The surgeon would be here later to see if his stitches were no longer needed. He would have to remember to gain the man's approval to be up and about. He did not wish to be scolded each time he attempted to venture from his room.

"However," he continued, "before I sat down, I did not bring the footstool near enough, and it would be more comfortable to sit with my feet up."

He had not even finished saying what he had to say before Lydia was crossing the room to move the footstool.

"I was going to ask that someone be sent to see to that," he told her.

"I am quite capable of moving a small piece of furniture, and I do not think it is improper to do so." She turned to Caroline. "Is it? Should I have summoned a servant?"

Miss Bingley shook her head and smiled. "Moving the footstool is perfectly acceptable. Being in a gentleman's bedroom is not."

Lydia gasped and scurried to the door. "Forgive me. I forgot."

To Richard's surprise, Miss Bingley smiled and said, "There is nothing to forgive. I was here to stand as chaperone. Your reputation is safe."

"What are you two doing this afternoon?" Richard asked.

"I am continuing my lessons. We have just completed the duties of the footmen and maids," Lydia replied. "There is a lot to remember, but Miss Bingley is very patient. Surprisingly so."

"Is that so?" Amusement had been so far from Richard for so many weeks that it was quite refreshing to feel it now.

"Oh, yes," she assured him seriously. "I fear I had a very incorrect view of who Miss Bingley was. She is not so cross as I had thought when I first met her. She is actually very pleasant, and I hope she will count me as a friend."

"I *was* cross when you met me," Caroline admitted. "I did not wish to be here. I preferred town."

"Do you still prefer town?" Lydia asked.

Caroline nodded. "To a degree. However, I find that the country improves when the company improves." She smiled. "I am most happy to be wherever Sir Matthew is."

"There are two chairs in here," Richard offered. "If you were both to join me, there would be nothing improper. I would like to hear how you and Sir Matthew are getting on."

Caroline's brow furrowed. "You would?"

"I am dreadfully bored, Miss Bingley."

"Very well, then, I suppose Miss Lydia and I can conclude our lesson for today."

"But will I know enough before any other guests arrive?" Lydia questioned as she entered the room. "I should hate to be found wanting."

"You will not be," Richard assured her.

"She most certainly will not be," Caroline agreed as she sat down on the small settee that was part of the furniture grouping before the hearth.

"This will not do," Lydia said, standing before Richard and extending her hand. "We must turn your chair. I refuse to speak to the side of your head."

Richard chuckled and lowered his feet, which he had just gotten comfortable on the footstool. Then, he took her hand and allowed her to assist him in standing.

"Stand here." She had pulled him three steps away from the chair.

"I can move the chair," he argued.

"And so can I," she replied with a bat of her lashes and a smile. "You will not deny me the pleasure of assisting you, will you?"

"No."

How could he refuse when she was looking at him so hopefully and with that particular look of delight? He understood precisely why Dash did whatever Lydia asked. Refusing her would take away that look and not even a pup like Dash, who was as unyielding as they came, could tolerate seeing such disappointment.

Speaking of the creature, Dash wandered into the room just at that moment and eyed Richard's chair.

"Absolutely not!" Lydia said firmly. "The rug is very comfortable, and the colonel must have this chair."

Dash's tale wagged as he listened to Lydia, and then as soon as she was done speaking, he sat down and waited for her to help Richard to his chair.

"Come here," Richard put a hand down in invitation to Dash, who willingly came to him for a scratch.

"Now, lie down," Lydia said, pointing to the rug.

Dash's head tipped and looked at the place where Lydia was pointing before lying down exactly where he was at Richard's side.

"Oh, very well, but do not disturb the colonel." Lydia moved the footstool into place before taking a seat next to Caroline.

"That is exactly what I mean,' Caroline said with a smile. "You knew precisely what was needed to make Colonel Fitzwilliam comfortable, and you were very direct in giving orders to Dash, even if he did not heed them completely.

"He'd be sacked if he were a footman," Richard teased.

"Perhaps not dismissed on the first instance," Lydia replied with a smile. "I would first speak to the butler and have him instruct the footman on what was and was not his place. A lowering of position could be tried first if the error did not correct itself. However," she sighed, "one must not have servants who are unwilling to do as they should."

"Well done, Miss Lydia," Caroline said. "You have been paying close attention."

"I wish to do well," Lydia answered.

"Why?" Richard asked.

He suspected he knew. Yesterday, they had not spoken of much except his injuries and how much they had missed each other in the few minutes of privacy Darcy had given them. And not all of those minutes had been used for talking either. Once he had convinced her that she would not injure him by kissing, there had been some time spent doing just that.

"As I said, I do not wish to be found wanting."

"By whom?"

"Well," she blinked her eyes as if surprised that he would ask such a thing, "by everyone. I should not wish for them to think you were unfortunately tied to an incapable or improper lady." She looked down at her hands. "Some might forbid you from courting me."

"I should like to see them try," he muttered.

Caroline took Lydia's hand. "If there is one thing that I have learned from Sir Matthew which I was never taught in school, it is that my success or failure is not judged by the opinions of strangers." She shrugged when Lydia looked at her in surprise. "You must first find yourself acceptable."

It was Richard's turn to blink. Caroline Bingley had always been concerned with the opinions of others for as long as he had known her. Was she no longer so enamoured with such?

"After that, it is only Sir Matthew's good opinion that I seek for I know that if I am pleased with myself and my effort, and he is equally as satisfied, then I have succeeded. Few others matter a great deal to my happiness."

"He is wise," Richard said.

"Excessively so," Caroline agreed.

Richard looked at Lydia. "Are you pleased with yourself?"

She shrugged. "I am not certain."

Caroline patted the hand she had been holding. "You will be. You only lack the confidence that comes with practice." She turned to Richard. "I was telling Miss Lydia just today when she arrived that I have decided to have her help me plan a dinner for when the countess is here. I will invite all the Bennets, and it will be an elaborate, festive affair." She smiled at Lydia who was looking a trifle uneasy. "It will be before your sisters are married and will be a celebration of their upcoming nuptials."

"That is an excellent idea," Richard said.

"We have not properly celebrated their betrothals," Caroline said.

"Nor have we celebrated yours," Lydia said.

"True! I think we should include you and Sir Matthew as honoured guests," Richard agreed heartily.

"But I am the hostess," Caroline deferred.

"Only one hostess. I believe you had another," Richard replied.

"I would prefer to not be celebrated." Caroline's

cheeks flushed. "Being promised to Sir Matthew is enough. I came into this betrothal..." She paused. "My behaviour was deplorable."

"I will not press the matter," Lydia said quietly. "If you do not wish it, it shall not be."

"I wish," Caroline whispered while glancing at the door as if checking to make certain they were alone. "I wish to prove myself as a gracious hostess and acquit myself as a proper sister who is happy for her brother and his friend."

"Ah. You wish to prove yourself," Richard said.

Caroline nodded. "Do not tell anyone else. Only Sir Matthew will know beyond us."

"Of course, you may trust us," Lydia assured her. "What are friends for if not to be trusted with secrets?"

"When I first arrived at Netherfield in the autumn, I never thought that you and I would be friends," Caroline said to Lydia.

"It is most remarkable, is it not?" Lydia agreed.

"Indubitably," Richard muttered.

Dash's head popped up as a cat crept into the room, slinking stealthily along the door.

"Have you met Oliver?" Lydia asked when she had spotted the cause for Dash's attention.

"Yes, Bingley introduced him to me."

"He and Dash are not yet friends."

Richard chuckled as he watched Oliver move around the room, carefully keeping his distance from Dash.

"The surgeon is here, sir," Richard's man stood at the door to his room. "He is waiting downstairs."

"I will see him in three minutes," Richard replied.

Caroline rose, and Lydia followed suit.

"Might I have a moment with Miss Lydia?" he asked Caroline.

"If the door is left open, I think it can be permitted," she agreed.

"Come closer," he said to Lydia as Caroline left the room. "Give me your hand."

Lydia held out her hand to him, and taking it, he bent to kiss it. "I need you to know that you will never be found wanting by me. No matter what anyone else might say. I love you."

She ducked her head and blushed sweetly. How he wished he was able-bodied enough to stand and embrace her.

Lifting her eyes to his, she held his gaze and said, "And I need you to know that to me you shall always be enough. No matter if your coat is red, blue, black, or green." Her brow furrowed. "I am actually rather fond of blue," she said with a playful smile that made him chuckle.

"It matters not what your profession or if you can only ever see me when I stand on this side of you, for I love you. Before I saw you yesterday, I did not know if I could love a gentleman who was not handsome."

Richard's eyes grew wide. She did not find him handsome? That was a bit of a blow.

"But I did not even think about how you looked beyond the fact that my heart broke for the pain you must have suffered." She bent and kissed his lips. "And I worried for nothing. You are quite as handsome as you have always been." She ran a finger lightly down his scar, causing it to tingle as the nerves attempted to come to life. "You are just now more distinguished."

"Kiss me again."

"It is highly improper, Colonel."

However, despite her protest, she did as he asked before leaving him to wait for the surgeon.

Chapter 19

"It is good to see you in the drawing room." Darcy looked up from the book he was reading as Richard entered the room with his brother standing watchfully at his side.

"I hear Mother is to arrive. I thought it best to look as fit as possible so that she would not send for every doctor in London."

"And a few from other locales," Westonbury quipped.

Lady Matlock had never been one to just allow her children to recuperate *as the good Lord deemed*, as her husband said it. As certain as her husband was about the fact that medication and doctors were not needed for every ailment, she was equally as certain that if doctors and medication were not needed then the good Lord would not have allowed them to exist. Therefore, if her children did not regain their health and vigour within a specified window of time – more or less mutually agreed upon between Lord and Lady Matlock – a physician would be sought.

"In fact, she might have one or two with her when she comes," Westonbury added as he took a seat after making sure that his brother was comfortable.

"With any luck, it will only be one," Richard agreed with a half smile. "There is nothing that can be done for me that has not already been done. And so, here I am, and I would appreciate it if you would not hover so much, Wes. Mother will think I am unwell if you do."

"Have you seen yourself?" Westonbury retorted. "She will think you are unwell whether or not I am watching to make sure you do not harm yourself in your haste to ignore your current condition."

The room was spinning again, and the sunlight shone more brightly in this room than in his bedroom. Richard closed his eyes. That would help. "I am not ignoring my condition. It will not allow me the pleasure, I assure you. However, I refuse to be limited by it completely. There is a lady..." He opened his good eye and peeked around the room as best he could. No one had joined them. It was just he, his brother, and Darcy. "There is a lady I should like to one day marry. Now, that I am free of my commission, I thought it would be good to consider marrying."

Not that he knew what he was going to do rather than command a group of men. But, without the ability to see what was beside him, he was of no use to them.

"Are you certain you are rid of it?" Darcy asked.

Again, Richard opened his good eye so that he could peek at his cousin. "I suspect so. The spinning has begun to improve, but my vision has not."

"And you fear it never will?" Darcy asked.

"Yes. As did the surgeon when I asked him."

"Ah! But that was just a country surgeon and not a physician from town," Westonbury said with a laugh.

Richard sighed. "I will consult such a person when I return to town if Mother has not stashed one in her trunk." He almost hoped that his mother had brought a doctor with her. He would like to hear what his fate would be from more than one source. It was not that he doubted the surgeon. He just did not wish to believe the man.

"Are we expecting other guests today?" Westonbury asked eagerly.

"Yes," Darcy answered. "I believe at least four of the Bennet sisters are intending to call."

"Only four?" Westonbury sounded disappointed.

"You may have to content yourself with tormenting Oliver," Darcy said dryly.

"That cat can climb all the way to the top of the drapery on that window behind you, Richard."

"Why you are proud of that fact, I do not understand. Pricks and snags from a kitten's claws do not add value to the fabric," Darcy chided.

Richard had heard how Westonbury had clapped his hands close to Oliver, and the startled creature had scurried up the drapes.

"It is almost as if Miss Mary is here," Westonbury teased Darcy.

"You should take up my commission," Richard muttered.

"We would be speaking French if he did," Darcy said.

"He needs something to do. Idleness only leads to mischief," Richard replied.

"He has an estate and eventually will have Mat-lock and all its duties."

"I do bore rather easily," Westonbury agreed. "There are no soirees here. There is no park in which to see and be seen. It is very dull, except when the Bennet ladies call."

His lips curled upward in pleasure but not as Richard had seen before. There was a peace to the smile where usually there was restlessness. Wes was always restless. Richard could not put his finger on it, but it was as if his brother viewed the arrival of the Bennets as something more than just a balm to boredom.

"There is to be a dinner tomorrow." Richard had heard about it from Lydia.

For the past three days since she and Caroline had visited with him for that first time in his room, she had spent at least an hour with him, reading to him or telling him about all the preparations.

"Yes, I am looking forward to it," Westonbury replied. "I hear there will be music afterward and then we will play cards. Georgie has some new song she is preparing."

"As does Miss Kitty," Darcy added.

"Both are doing very well." He sighed. "Miss Mary refuses to play."

"Does she? I thought I had heard her practising with Georgiana one day," Darcy said.

"Very well. She only refuses to play when I am in the room or even in the corridor. She makes Kitty stand guard at the door."

Richard chuckled. "She banishes you from the music room?"

"She'd likely banish me from England if she could."

Richard's head tipped at his brother's curiously perturbed tone.

"And why is that?" he asked.

Westonbury blew out a breath. "Something about Sally's. It is not on the list of Miss Mary approved places or activities."

"Which is as it should be," Darcy muttered.

"Do you know what she said to me on our walk the day I met her?"

"I am sure I could not even guess," Richard replied. He knew, however, that something said in the exchange between the two had made an impression on his brother. Darcy had said so. And as far as Richard knew, Darcy had still not discovered what had been said between the two. Elizabeth had not told him, though she knew. Apparently, it was not the sort of thing Elizabeth wished to repeat. Nor was it the sort of thing Darcy would press to discover. Darcy was patient where Richard was curious. Richard had thought to ask Lydia about it but had not.

"That places such as Sally's only exist because of men – she did not say gentlemen, she said men – such as me who have no care for anyone but themselves." He rose from where he was sitting and scooped up Oliver before he could escape. "That was the end of our disagreement thanks to Miss Lydia." He sat down again and pulled out his watch fob to dangle in front of the kitten in his lap. "Apparently, there are men of honour such as you, Darcy, and even father – since none of you frequent such a place as Sally's – however, I am not to be counted amongst that number." He looked up from Oliver to Richard. "Is she always so severe and set in her opinions?"

"I could not say," Richard replied.

"I believe she is. Elizabeth said it would take a

heroic deed to sway her opinion once it is so firmly set against someone," Darcy inserted.

The statement was met by a short burst of laughter from Westonbury. "Perhaps I do need to take up your commission after all."

"Perhaps if you started by not provoking her?" Darcy suggested.

Westonbury sighed. "Perhaps."

"We are not children any longer, Wes. You cannot throw pebbles at the girls you like," Richard said.

Understanding dawned in Darcy's eyes. "Oh, yes! I remember you used to torment any girl who caught your fancy. Do you like Miss Mary?"

"No. Yes. I do not know. I only know that it bothers me greatly that she thinks so poorly of me and that her opinion was set before she even met me. Should I not, at least, be given a chance to make a first impression?"

"Miss Bennet, Miss Elizabeth Bennet, and Miss Lydia Bennet," Mr. Harvey intoned from the doorway.

With some effort not to grimace, Richard pushed up from his seat.

"Colonel," Elizabeth said, "it is good to see you in the drawing room."

"You helped him come down; did you not?" Lydia asked Westonbury.

"I promised you I would," he replied.

"Then show me your cheek," she answered.

"You will not pinch my nose, will you?"

She laughed. "Is it necessary?"

"No." He turned his cheek towards her, and she kissed it.

"Thank you. You are a very good brother."

Richard could almost imagine her patting Wes on the head and giving him a biscuit as she did Dash. "You only helped me for a kiss?"

Westonbury shrugged and smirked. "Can you blame me? I am to keep my half-crowns to myself, after all."

"I did not say I would give him a kiss when he promised to see to you," Lydia said, folding her arms and joining Richard in glaring at his brother.

"She is correct. I was never promised a reward for making certain you did not fall to your death on the stairs."

"And he only got a kiss because there is no one here who would think it utterly improper."

"Speaking of which. Where is Miss Mary?" Westonbury asked. "She might like to know that I performed my duty as brother so admirably."

Lydia laughed. "She is in the music room with Kitty and Georgiana. I will be certain to tell her, but I fear she will still not like you. You did buy a kiss from her sister."

Westonbury's mouth dropped open. "Is that why she does not like me?"

"That and you were at Sally's," Lydia said. "What else could it be? That is all she knew of you before she met you."

"I did not know she knew of that kiss," Elizabeth said.

"Oh, she was not supposed to know, but I forgot and mentioned it on that day when Lord Westonbury arrived. I was so shocked that he was the same person we had met at Sally's that I had to tell Kitty and well, Mary happened to be there when I did," Lydia answered.

"That does make things fall into place better," Jane said.

"Miss Bennet!" Bingley said as he entered the room. "I am delighted to see you. My sister has

220

given me permission to enter," he added to Miss Lydia.

"What do you mean *given you permission?*" Richard asked. "This is your house. Why would you need permission to enter your own drawing room."

"You do not need to be overwhelmed the first time you are out of your room," Lydia answered. "That is why Caroline and I decided that you should be given time to get settled here without too many people or too much sound."

Westonbury laughed. "You do not need Mother. It seems Miss Lydia is filling the role of protectress very well."

Richard watched Lydia pull the right corner of her lower lip between her teeth. He also saw Darcy sit forward as if he wished to move in and care for Lydia, but then he move back purposefully and nodded to Richard. It was what he did when he thought Richard needed to address Georgiana. Lydia had become very much a sister to his cousin, and Richard would not disappoint either him or Lydia.

"I believe Mother would be delighted to know

someone has seen to my care," Richard assured her.

"Do you think so?" Lydia asked eagerly.

"Yes," Westonbury said. "Do you think Miss Mary would let me hear her play today?"

"I doubt it very much," Lydia answered.

He sighed and settled back into his chair.

"Is all ready for tomorrow evening?" Richard asked.

Lydia nodded. "I have just to practice my song."

"Your song?"

She nodded again.

"I did not know you were singing."

"It is supposed to be a surprise, so I shall not tell you any more than that." Her head tipped. "Do you think your head can abide listening to several songs? You will already have endured a dinner."

"I would not miss such a treat as hearing you sing. Even if I must do it with my eyes closed to keep the room from spinning. I will imagine your lovely face if I must close my eyes," he added when her brow furrowed.

"Lady Matlock's carriage is on the drive," Harvey said from the doorway. "Miss Bingley wished you to know in advance of her arrival. Tea will be made ready soon."

Lydia's hands twisted in her lap, and Richard covered them with one of his. "All will be well. You are prepared. She might be surly at first, but she will be won over."

He had said these same words to her every day she had visited him in his room, but at present, the words felt a great deal weightier much like "you know your post, see to it" took on a far different tone when said in the face of battle rather than field practice.

"It might be a challenge, but you are equal to it," he added.

She nodded, and, upon hearing Netherfield's door open, she rose and then assisted him in also rising. Her shoulders straightened, and she lifted her chin. His Lydia was prepared for whatever lay ahead. He gave her hand a squeeze before releasing it.

"You are equal to it," he whispered once more before his mother was announced.

Chapter 20

Lady Matlock surveyed the room, her eyes taking in every detail. It was not an unfamiliar action to Darcy. It was how his aunt entered all new rooms.

Her left brow quirked upward as she settled her gaze on him.

"Mother," Westonbury said. "May I present the room to you?"

"I believe you must, my dear. There are those here whom I have not yet met." She spoke sweetly but her eyes remained on Darcy.

"It was not feasible for you to meet them when they were in town. Lord Matlock agreed," Darcy said in answer to her look.

"Yes, well, he is not as curious as I am." She had the good grace to smile at Elizabeth. "Begin here," she said to Westonbury.

"Mother this is Fitz—"

"Oh, do skip over the people I know, Reginald." She huffed. "Why must you insist on being such a trial?"

"Because I am much like you?"

"Reginald Arthur Fitzwilliam, do your duty as you should," Lady Matlock retorted.

Westonbury chuckled. "My full name and not even five minutes have passed. That must be a record."

"Indeed," his mother replied dryly but with a smile for her eldest son. "Now, get on with it. And do it properly."

"Lady Matlock, I present to you Miss Elizabeth Bennet, soon to be Mrs. Elizabeth Darcy. Miss Elizabeth, my mother, Lady Matlock."

Elizabeth dipped a curtsey. "It is a pleasure to meet you."

"Oh, do not assume things," Lady Matlock replied with a small laugh. "Reginald was not wrong. We can be alike – difficult and trying."

"I am not unused to trying and difficult people," Elizabeth returned with a smile.

"I should think not if you have agreed to take on Darcy."

Darcy cleared his throat and scowled.

"You are so exacting, and do not tell me you are not." She turned to Westonbury. "Continue, and I do know Mr. Bingley. I should very much like to know who the beauty is beside him."

"Lady Matlock, I present to you Miss Jane Bennet, soon to be Mrs. Jane Bingley. Miss Bennet, my mother, Lady Matlock."

Jane also dipped a curtsey as was proper and voiced her pleasure in Lady Matlock's safe arrival.

"A gentleman's daughter?" she directed the question to Bingley, who nodded. "Excellent. That is just what you need to help establish yourself." She tipped her head and studied Jane for a moment. "And strikingly pretty. Make sure to have her likeness captured in a portrait," she instructed Bingley before looking once again at Westonbury.

"Lady Matlock, I present to you Miss Lydia Bennet. Miss Lydia, this is my mother, Lady Matlock."

As Darcy expected, Lydia dipped a curtsey.

"No, soon to be Mrs. Anybody?" Lady Matlock said over Lydia's greeting.

"No, my lady," Lydia answered.

"Not soon at least," Richard answered, causing Lydia's eyes to grow wide. "But I am hopeful."

Lady Matlock lifted her chin and swept her eyes

from Lydia's head to her feet and back. "A trifle young, do you not think?"

"No," Richard replied. "She is perfect in every way."

"I am not," Lydia said.

"To me you are," Richard assured her.

Lady Matlock's lips twitched as if she wished to smile. "I have been attempting to bring him to the point of marriage." She blew out a breath. "However, he is stubborn." She began to peel off her gloves. "You are not what I would expect." She held up a finger to keep Richard from saying anything. "That being said, I will not discount you straight away. Someone of your age might in time learn the fortitude necessary for such a stubborn husband." She handed the first of her gloves to Westonbury and began removing the second glove. "He is a lot like his father. And, though I know you are a gentleman's daughter, the circles in which he is expected to circulate are not those to which you are accustomed." She handed the second glove to Westonbury and looked at Lydia expectantly.

Lydia's chin rose, but only just. "I believe that when my sister spoke of not being unfamiliar with trying individuals, she was thinking, at least in part, about me."

"Indeed?" Lady Matlock looked toward Elizabeth who nodded. "And only this one sister is trying?"

"No, my lady," Lydia answered for Elizabeth. "Jane is all that is good, as is Kitty, but Lizzy, Mary and myself are more challenging."

"Five sisters?" Lady Matlock blinked.

"Yes, my lady," Lydia said. "No brothers. My father's estate is entailed to his cousin, who holds the living in Hunsford, and my mother's family is from trade." She batted her lashes and smiled.

Darcy's eyes grew wide. From all the nervousness he had witnessed in Lydia over the past few days as the arrival of his aunt grew closer and closer, he had not expected such a bold reply. He wanted to look at Elizabeth to see how she was reacting to Lydia's outspoken behaviour, but he dared not take his eyes off his aunt, for he was curious to witness her response.

"And do you know how to manage a large household?" Lady Matlock countered.

"My mother is very good at what she does, my lady," Lydia responded. "And she has instructed me well. However, I have also requested and received instruction by Miss Bingley to ensure that my skills are not lacking since Miss Bingley is more familiar with town than is my mother."

Truly, Darcy had not expected her to admit that either.

"A Bennet always rises to the occasion," Elizabeth whispered.

He glanced her direction.

"Not that I am not also shocked by it," she added.

"And where are these other sisters?" Lady Matlock asked.

"They are with Georgiana in the music room," Darcy answered.

"I can take you there and introduce them to you," Westonbury offered.

"No!" Darcy said sharply.

Lady Matlock turned startled eyes to him. "And why can he not?"

"They are practising," Darcy answered.

"They can pause to meet me."

"Then, it would be best if I were to take you to them."

"Is there a reason for this?" She looked at Westonbury, who shrugged.

Darcy smiled apologetically at Lydia. "Wes and Miss Mary do not get on well together."

"Have you been tormenting the poor girl, Reginald?"

"He gets as good as he gives," Darcy supplied.

"I see. Well, then, we will wait for introductions until later." She finally took a seat.

Lydia took Richard by the elbow and assisted him in sitting, making certain he was comfortable before she took her place next to him.

"I have asked Mr. Westcott to see you," Lady Matlock said to Richard. "He was not available until the day after tomorrow, however, so he will arrive with your father. Your father cannot stay for very long, but he did wish to see you."

"I can wait until I return to London to see Mr. Westcott," Richard replied.

"Oh, but he is so very good," Lydia said. "He tended to my father when he fell," she explained to Lady Matlock. "Papa only spoke well of him, so he must be very good." She turned back to Richard. "And it is never a bad thing to seek another's opinion, is it?" Her head tipped and her lashes fluttered.

Richard scowled. "I suppose it is not."

"And you will not be returning to London until after the wedding," Lydia added. "So, seeing Mr. Westcott now rather than later would be a good thing, would it not be?"

Richard closed his eyes.

"He might know more about how to help you," Lydia added, "or if there is anything more that you should be doing to recover."

Again, her lashes fluttered when Richard opened his eyes, and Darcy knew that is cousin was doomed to agree to have Mr. Westcott visit.

"You are correct," Richard muttered.

Lady Matlock smiled. "You might work out after all," she said. "However, I will reserve my approval for now until I have observed further."

The door to the drawing room opened, allowing Caroline, accompanied by Sir Matthew and the tea service, to enter. Introductions were made, and Lydia was called upon to help pour.

~*~*~

"That went better than I expected," Elizabeth admitted to Darcy later as they were taking a walk around the garden.

She would have to leave soon, but at his insistence, her departure had been put off for the length of a slow walk around the hedges and flower beds.

"It most certainly did," Darcy replied. "I must say I was surprised by how accepting my aunt was of everyone."

"You mean Lydia?"

"Yes, and you, to some extend, but mostly Lydia. My aunt has long spoken about how she wished to see Richard marry an heiress." It was odd really how easily his aunt had accepted Lydia. She had not even raised a brow at Mrs. Bennet being from trade. Whatever the cause of her behavior was, Darcy was happy for it. "She may have been swayed by Lydia's boldness. My aunt does not favour wilting wallflowers – that is what she calls them. A lady should be decorous but with a spine of iron."

Elizabeth laughed and hugged Darcy's arm more tightly. "Well, Lydia does have a will of iron at times, and she is working on being decorous."

Darcy kissed the top of Elizabeth's bonnet. "I am impressed by the change I have seen in her. Yesterday, she was sitting with Mrs. Annesley asking questions about a great number of things for a time, or so Georgiana told me."

"I am just as surprised by her improvement as you are, if not more so," Elizabeth said. "I should not be, I suppose, but I am."

Darcy led Elizabeth off the main path and over the lawn toward a bench across from where they had been walking. "Why should you not be surprised?"

"Lydia has always found a way to get what she wants. She wants the colonel's good opinion, and so, she will do whatever is needed to gain and keep it. I had not thought of that until recently." She sighed.

"What troubles you?"

"I have been blind to so many things."

"Such as?"

"Such as Caroline is not without sense and is very accomplished."

"She hid her sense rather well for some time. I do not think you can be faulted for not noticing it. In fact, I dare say if she did not have Sir Matthew, she would still be rather nonsensical, though possessing many accomplishments. What else?"

"Lydia is not a child."

"I think her experiences of late have played a large role in her maturity," Darcy countered.

Elizabeth shrugged. "I guess I view things through a different lens now than I did before I went to London."

"Life is changing," Darcy said softly. "And not for the worse."

"Definitely not for the worse," Elizabeth agreed, lifting her face so he could kiss her.

"I have requested permission of your father for your sisters to visit Georgiana after we marry."

"You did what?"

Darcy smiled sheepishly. "Georgiana has grown so close to them."

Elizabeth shook her head and laughed softly. "Where has the old Mr. Darcy gone?"

"The one who did not see your worth and denied his heart? He is gone. You do not wish for him to return, do you?" He kissed her upturned lips again.

"No, but my sisters? Was not two weeks enough trial?"

He chuckled. "I think I can survive another fortnight or two."

"And has my father agreed?"

"In part. Georgiana is going to stay at Long-bourn for two weeks after we leave. Then, Lydia and Kitty are to join us for a time. One for my cousin's sake and the other for my sister's." He blew out a breath. "I offered to have Mary accompany them, but your father has not decided. He might send her to your aunt's, or he might keep her at home for your mother. I believe it is the animosity between Wes and Mary which causes him to pause."

"For good reason." A creased formed between Elizabeth's eyes. "Do you not fear leaving your sister where Mr. Wickham is?"

Darcy shook his head. "Your mother – and Lydia – will not allow him to harm her." He stroked her cheek. "I never thought I would relish being part of your family. I know that sounds arrogant, and it was when I first thought it. But now. I honestly cannot imagine my life without them." He tipped his head as he stroked her cheek once more before brushing her lips with his thumb. "We do not need to stay in town for long after we marry. We could have everyone join us at Pemberley."

"Mother does not like to travel, and Jane will be here."

"We will think on it," he answered as his hand moved to cup the back of her head.

She smiled. "What has happened to your well-ordered life, Mr. Darcy?"

"It has been completely turned on its head," he replied, pulling her in for a kiss. "My heart has been broken open and filled with love for you and your family. I do not wish to have my former life back."

"And what has wrought this change?" she said as he lowered his head for a lingering kiss.

"Well," he said, "it began when you stole my heart." He kissed her again. "And over time and through challenges." Another kiss. "I learned to see beyond myself." One more kiss, this one on her nose. "However, I do believe that next to my great love for you, I would have to credit Dash for a great deal of it." He lowered his lips to hers. There was nothing in this world that he would not endure to be here with her, breathing in the lavender fragrance she wore, tasting the sweetness of her kisses, and reveling in her touch as she wound her arms around his neck.

Chapter 21

Two weeks passed quickly. Much more quickly than Darcy had expected they would. Lady Matlock's presence, as well as that of her husband on two separate occasions, had added a liveliness to life at Netherfield that had propelled time forward at a rapid pace. The drawing room had been filled with chatter and card games. Georgiana had been called upon to play more than once. Quietness was not something which Lady Matlock sought. She was, in fact, a rather restless soul much like her eldest son. However, the busyness and noise which filled Netherfield did not bother Darcy as it once might have. Indeed, if he were to be honest, he had missed such things since leaving town and found them to be a bit of a solace.

Darcy chuckled as he thought about these things while descending the stairs at Netherfield on his way to enter his carriage, which was waiting to take him to the church. He had learned a great deal from the Bennets about what it was to be part of a loving, though somewhat chaotic, family.

"You are looking handsome, as always," Lady Matlock greeted Darcy. She motioned for him to stand in front of her so that she could straighten his jacket, though it did not need it.

"Your mother would be pleased to see you so happy." She placed a hand on his cheek. "Your father, too, but I think a son's wedding day is more a time for mothers to be nostalgic than it is for fathers."

"I should think you are correct," Darcy replied. "I know I have thought more of my mother in the last week than my father, though both have been close to mind." He was sorry that neither of them would ever know Elizabeth and her family.

"You are not alone. My husband has mentioned his sister and your father both times when he was here." She looked around Darcy and up the stairs. "Is Georgiana travelling with you?"

"No, she will travel with Richard and Weston-bury." The seat next to him was reserved for Eliza-beth.

"Good, then you will have a place for me."

"But –" Darcy began to protest that he was not going to share his carriage with her after the ceremony was over, but she held up a hand to stop him.

"Your uncle will see me to the wedding breakfast. I will not come between you and your bride." She gave him a wink and a smirk that was so very reminiscent of her eldest son that Darcy could not help but chuckle.

"Very well, as long as I shall be alone with Elizabeth after we have said our vows, I will allow you to accompany me to the church."

"Such a good boy." She gave his cheek a pat. "If only my boys were so well behaved." Again, she winked and smirked.

Darcy knew that while there were most certainly times when she wished her sons were as reserved as he was, his aunt would not wish them to always be so. She could be as troublesome as either Richard or Westonbury.

Her smirk faded from her lips but not her eyes as she gave him an expectant look. Obediently, he extended his arm to her and led her from the house.

"I have not yet gotten to do this with either of

my boys," she said as they descended Netherfield's steps. "But," she added as they approached the carriage, "it seems I will sooner rather than later."

"How do you mean?"

Darcy was almost certain he understood his aunt's meaning. She had been very attentive to Lydia and had not had a critical thing to say. Whether she was simply keeping criticism to herself or truly approved was the true question, and frankly, it was one he had hoped to ask of her before he departed Netherfield later today.

The need to see that Lydia was well would not leave him, even if he had given over that responsibility to Richard for the past two weeks. It was only natural, he supposed since, as of today, Lydia would be his sister, and, as such, he would never truly stop worrying about her wellbeing.

"Richard spoke to his father last night," Lady Matlock said as she entered the carriage.

"Did he?" Darcy feigned surprise.

She turned and leveled a look of disbelief at him. "As if you do not know."

Darcy smiled. "I may have heard something about it."

"I am sure you heard all about it," she retorted.

"As you know, your uncle has given his blessing to Richard, and so I suspect in a year or perhaps sooner, I will get to take this ride with him." She settled into her seat. "There is no rush, however. Richard must heal and find his footing in a new life, and Miss Lydia is young."

Darcy could not have asked for a better opening to present his case for Lydia if one should be needed. He would fight for both her and Richard. His cousin was making remarkable progress since he had agreed to see Lydia. His mood had lifted, and his determination had resurged. Unfortunately, his eyesight had not cleared even though he was no longer as dizzy as he had been.

"Are you pleased about the match?"

His aunt drew a breath and expelled it before pursing her lips and looking out the window. "Truthfully, she is not what I expected." She shrugged. "But then, every well-dowered accomplished debutante I have paraded before him has only ever elicited a bored pleasantness from him. Miss Lydia is not boring." She smiled as if truly delighted by that fact.

"No, she is not that," Darcy agreed.

"She is full of vitality and stubbornness." His

aunt chuckled. She was obviously quite pleased with the lady whom her youngest son had selected as his future wife. "I suspect I always knew he would need someone different from what the best finishing schools produce. He is a lot like his father."

"He is, and you are not a standard issue ton-approved lady." That was how his uncle had always described his aunt when talking about what it was which had captured his interest when he had met his wife.

"No, I am not." She smiled. "Standard is boring." Again, she shrugged. "However, it is occasionally preferable to be boring. It draws fewer arrows." She had not been a part of the ton when she had met her husband.

"I believe Miss Lydia can withstand a few arrows," Darcy said. She had survived Richard's injury and seemingly had managed to win over Richard's mother, which was no small task.

Again, his aunt chuckled. "I do not doubt it, and much like his father did for me, Richard will pro-tect her where he can." She sighed. "I was so curi-ous to meet her after Lady Catherine told us about her, so it was a relief to have her here to greet me when I arrived two weeks ago."

"I beg your pardon?" Lady Catherine had spoken of Lydia? Why had Wes not said so?

His aunt looked at him in confusion.

"Wes said he learned about Miss Lydia from Mrs. Salter and not Aunt Catherine," Darcy explained.

Lady Matlock's eyebrows flew upward. "What does *that* woman know of Miss Lydia?"

"You know Mrs. Salter?"

Darcy pressed his lips together to keep from laughing at his aunt's unladylike description of the woman while replying in the affirmative that she did indeed know Mrs. Salter.

"Mrs. Salter was disappointed in her quest to snare Mr. Bennet when she was young. Lost him to a lady from trade."

Lady Matlock leaned forward. "Do tell."

"I cannot tell you the whole story. It is not mine to share. However, according to Wes, Mrs. Salter had heard that Richard and Miss Lydia had been seen out walking and had thought it would be an excellent thing if she could do one better than Mrs. Bennet and attach her daughter to Wes."

His aunt's eyes grew wide. "Not while I live," she snarled. "That woman is an annoyance. I will not have her be a part of this family." Her smile was a bit calculating.

Darcy was curious as to what made his aunt dislike Mrs. Salter so vehemently but having heard as many stories as he had about the woman, he was not surprised that she was not well-liked.

"Do you know she had the audacity to proclaim that no second son would be a first choice for her daughter?" his aunt said. Her look of contempt from the first mention of Mrs. Salter's name had not faded one bit.

"Where did she do this?"

"Oh, some musicale," she said with a wave of her hand. "It might have been at the Johnsons', although I am not entirely certain. Not that it matters where. It was one of those times when I was attempting to force Richard to meet several young ladies. I had not met Mrs. Salter before that evening. Well," she arched her left eyebrow and pursed her lips to emphasize the vileness of what she was about to share, "I was speaking to someone else when the mother of one of the young ladies I had introduced to Richard was talking to Mrs.

Salter about her excitement at her daughter meeting the son of Lord Matlock." Lady Matlock lifted her chin. "As any sensible mother should be. Being tied to Lord Matlock is no small thing – even if it is through his second son and not his first." Her eyes narrowed. "As if one is better than the other. Oh, I know one has a title and will have a fortune, but Richard is not a prize to be snubbed."

Darcy smiled. His aunt had always loved her children fiercely.

"Well, any woman who can dismiss my son, is not worth my time or notice!" Her lips curled into a calculating smirk. "I think I shall have to invite Miss Lydia to see the town with me when she visits. Would that not just put a bee in Mrs. Salter's bonnet."

"Indeed, it would," Darcy agreed. "But back to Aunt Catherine. You said she told you about Miss Lydia?"

Lady Matlock nodded. "She felt it her duty to tell your uncle and me about the fiery young lady she had met at Netherfield who claimed to be loved by Richard." She blew out a breath. "We were shocked at first, of course, since we had heard nothing about Miss Lydia or any attachment

Richard had formed. And to be honest, we had always thought he would marry an heiress to prop up his inheritance a shade or two. It was what he had always claimed he would do, you know. However, after Lady Catherine cautioned us that no disparagement of the young woman would be allowed by you, I knew this Miss Lydia must be a quality young lady."

It was gratifying that Lady Catherine had taken his words to heart. He was not anxious to create a breach in the family, but he would have, had she not heeded his warning. "She is my sister – or will be soon. How could I do otherwise?"

His aunt shook her head. "If Miss Lydia had been a poor choice for Richard to be making, you would have attempted to sway him. You have always watched out for him. It is just part of your nature to do so. That things had progressed enough for Miss Lydia to know that Richard loved her proved that you more than tolerated her. You approved."

"I was not certain I would at first," Darcy admitted. "It was Richard who saw the potential in her from their first meeting when she asked him if he was married."

"She did not!"

"Oh, she did. She also asked if Georgiana had any beaus."

"Miss Lydia? I find that hard to believe."

"That is because she has improved, just as Richard set out to help her do before his heart became entangled — or perhaps it was as it became entangled. The Bennet ladies seem to have a power to charm a fellow rather quickly."

"They are charming, even Miss Mary when she is scowling at Reginald," his aunt said with a chuckle. "There mother is... well, she is loving despite her deficits." Her brows flicked up quickly in amusement.

"She is," Darcy agreed. Mrs. Bennet was still not an excessively intelligent woman. She was still given to rattling on in conversations and taking the longest route around a point while sometimes missing the point altogether. However, Darcy found he did not fault her for those things as he once did. "I am pleased she will be my mother-in-law." And he meant it.

"She will treat you well."

"I have no doubt of that." He moved toward the door as it was opened.

"I cannot believe you are finally getting married," his aunt said as she allowed him to help her out of the carriage.

"I am a bit in shock over that as well," Darcy replied with a chuckle.

Darcy's wedding day had been a long time in coming, and for a long, bleak time, it had appeared that such happiness as he now felt would never be his. However, as he stood here before the church ready to claim his bride, those days of sorrow seemed to fade nearly into nonexistence. It was almost as if they had been but a fitful night of sleep, disturbed by countless bad dreams.

While Darcy's journey to his wedding day had been a long one, the ceremony was, as it always is, over in what seemed like a moment, and the journey between Netherfield and the church? Well, when one was agreeably engaged in kissing and holding his wife rather than talking to his aunt, a few miles seemed more like a few feet, and the journey was rather disappointingly over far sooner than Darcy wished for it to be.

Chapter 22

"Your mother and Caroline have outdone themselves," Darcy said as he entered the ballroom at Netherfield, which had been laid out for a lavish wedding breakfast.

There were flowers lining the center of the tables, weaving in and around platters and bowls. Glasses sparkled as they stood alongside fine china and well-polished silver. There were even ribbons tied to the chairs intended for the guests of honour.

"And Lydia. We must not forget Lydia. She has been helping Caroline," Elizabeth reminded him.

"Was this during Richard's required rest period?" Darcy still found it humorous that his cousin – a well-respected colonel in his majesty's armed forces, who was used to giving commands and having them immediately obeyed on pain of punishment, was so easily talked into spending an hour of his time alone in his room by a flutter of lashes and a pretty pout on a determined young lady.

Elizabeth laughed. "Yes, it was while the colonel was resting. I heard about each day's progress every night at dinner."

Elizabeth glanced toward where Richard was already seated at the end of the head table, near a door through which he could make a hasty exit if needed. Lydia had insisted upon him sitting there. She was not about to allow him to become overwhelmed where one and all would notice. "They make such a good pair, do they not?"

Darcy could not agree more. His cousin was happy — utterly happy despite his injuries — and that happiness was due almost entirely to the young lady whispering something to him right at this moment.

"Then, you are no longer fearful that such a relationship will end in tragedy as you once were?"

Elizabeth sighed. "There are some things which you should likely not remember."

"Such as any time you were wrong?" he teased.

"Yes," Elizbeth replied quickly, "but that should

not be hard to do since I am so very nearly always right." She looked up at him and favoured him with an impertinent grin as he stood behind her chair while she took her seat at the table near the front of the room.

Leaning down, he kissed her. How could he not when she looked so charming, especially now that she was his wife?

"Mr. Darcy, how improper!" Jane was just taking her place next to her sister.

"But an excellent idea," Bingley said, placing a kiss on Jane's cheek since she was looking at Elizabeth.

"Shall we cause a scandal?" Jane said, turning toward her new husband.

"It would not be the first," he replied before kissing her properly.

"Such changes!" Elizabeth cried. "Who would have thought that Mr. Darcy and my best-behaved sister would become such wanton individuals?"

"What about me?" Bingley said when their laughter had died some. "Are you not shocked by my behaviour?"

"No."

"No? I am wounded." He placed a hand on his heart.

Elizabeth leaned forward and looked around her sister to Bingley. "You are not as reserved as they are. However, I must say I was shocked to hear you had cut ties with your sister. Shocked and excessively pleased. Jane is worth a bit of trouble."

"I could not agree more," Bingley said.

"And her sister is worth even more trouble." Darcy wrapped an arm around Elizabeth's shoulder and squeezed her tightly to his side.

"The things you have endured," Elizabeth teased.

From lending a hand in staging a compromise to hosting her family at his house to mingling with them and their friends and neighbors here in Hertfordshire, there had been much which could have been a step too far from comfort had the prize been anything less than the lady sitting beside Darcy. However, only one of them had proven excessively difficult to endure.

"Not a one was too much except for that one night when you were missing."

But then, that one thing — Darcy's fear of losing her, even when it was simply a fear of never gaining her approval, and therefore, living in misery without her — had been the impetus to all that had happened in the past few months.

Mr. Bennet stood and tapped his glass with his knife, drawing everyone's attention and causing a hush to fall over the room.

"It is with pleasure," he began, "that I welcome two sons to my family today. Please, join me on this happy occasion in raising a glass to the happiness, health, and –"

"Prosperity," Mrs. Bennet inserted, causing a titter of laughter to spread around the room.

"Yes, prosperity," Mr. Bennet agreed. "May my daughters and their husbands prosper in love as they grow older and may their homes always be filled with as much love and laughter as mine has always been." He lifted his glass. "To the Darcys and Bingleys!"

A cheer was raised around the room, followed by the clinking of glass against glass.

"I have enjoyed this day so much," Mr. Bennet said when the room had once again stilled, "that I would not be opposed to doing it again." He nodded to Richard before returning his attention to the room at large.

"I still have two daughters yet unattached," he added, once again causing the room to laugh. "And Darcy has a sister, we must not forget Miss Darcy. It is, after all," he said with a smile for his wife, "a truth universally acknowledged that young ladies such as Kitty, Mary, and Miss Darcy, who are in possession of great beauty and generally sweet spirits, must be in want of husbands."

Mrs. Bennet gasped and clucked her tongue softly before tittering behind her wine goblet as the rest of the room also chuckled.

"I have one more duty to perform before I will allow you all to eat and be merry as is required on a day such as this. My youngest, along with the assistance of Miss Darcy, has prepared some music to start us off while we eat."

"Did you know about this? Did Georgiana tell you?" Elizabeth whispered to Darcy.

"I did know about it, but it was not Georgie who told me."

"It was not?"

Darcy shook his head.

"Miss Darcy, Lydia," Mr. Bennet motioned to the piano which had been placed in the far corner. "We look forward to hearing what you have prepared, my dear," he said to Lydia, "and we shall all pretend that it is only in honor of your sisters and not a certain colonel."

"Papa!" Lydia chided, her cheeks growing red. "It can be for everyone."

"Of course, my dear, of course," he said as he took his seat.

"Your sister did not get to sing her song the night of the dinner party for Lady Matlock," Darcy whispered.

"You mean she refused," Elizabeth corrected.

"Because Richard was absent," Darcy reminded her. "So, she asked me if I thought it would be a good idea to sing it here."

"She did?" Elizabeth's face was suffused with shock.

Darcy nodded. "Apparently, she values my opinion," he teased, earning him a roll of Elizabeth's fine eyes. "When I heard her reason for wishing to perform here today, I could not say no. It is an excellent song choice."

"Is it? You know which song she was to sing at that dinner party? She has been very guarded about it."

Darcy smiled. "I do know. Now, do you wish to know her reason?"

"Of course."

"She wanted to make a very public declaration that Richard is and always will be good enough for her."

"What is she singing?" Elizabeth's eyes were wide.

Darcy shook his head. "That I will not tell you. You must listen to discover it, and as you do, know that I would say the same to you – which is precisely what I told your sister when we discussed this. She knows that she is not just singing for herself but also for me." Miss Lydia had required a handkerchief after hearing him speak so about the sister who had been such a wonderful support to her ever since that night at Sally's.

Of course, her declaration of delight over his attachment to her sister had come at the expense of hearing how shocked she still was that he was not so horrid as she had first thought he was. It was not so painful a thing to be reminded of his poor behavior now as it might have been at one time. However, it would be far better to be able to forget such a thing than to be reminded of it. He lifted

Elizabeth's hand to his lips as the first notes rang out from the piano.

"Lydia looks so calm," Elizabeth whispered.

"Love has that sort of effect on one. It is truly astounding what one would not normally do for the world but will gladly do in a heartbeat for love." He placed a kiss on the ear into which he had whispered.

Next to the piano, Lydia lifted her chin and smiled first at Elizabeth and Jane before turning her attention to Colonel Fitzwilliam as she began to sing.

Believe me, if all those endearing young charms,
Which I gaze on so fondly to-day,
Were to change by to-morrow, and fleet in my arms,
Live fairy-gifts fading away,
Thou wouldst still be adored, as this moment thou art,
Let thy loveliness fade as it will,
And around the dear ruin each wish of my heart
Would entwine itself verdantly still.

Elizabeth drew in a sharp breath, and her hand rose to cover her heart. Turning to Darcy, tears glistening in her eyes, she whispered, "It is so beautiful and perfect. So perfect."

"Indeed, it is, for I love you, Mrs. Darcy, and I

always will." He was certain Elizabeth would have replied in kind if he had allowed it. However, he did not, for he could not refrain from kissing her as Lydia began the last verse.

It is not while beauty and youth are thine own,
And thy cheeks unprofaned by a tear,
That the fervor and faith of a soul may be known,
To which time will but make thee more dear!
No, the heart that has truly loved never forgets,
But as truly loves on to the close,
As the sunflower turns on her god when he sets
The same look which she turned when he rose![1]

Today, tomorrow, next year, and until time ceased to exist, Darcy would only love Elizabeth more than he did at this moment. And when he broke their kiss far sooner than he wished and as she laid her head on his shoulder, he knew that, by marrying Elizabeth, his greatest achievement in his life had both been reached and had only begun to be grasped.

---

1. *Believe Me if All Those Endearing Young Charms, Thomas Moore*

Before You Go

If you enjoyed this book, be sure to let others
know by leaving a review.
~*~*~
Want to know when other books in this series
will be available?
You can always know what's new with my
books by subscribing to my mailing list.
(There will, of course, be a thank you gift for
joining because I think my readers are awesome!)
Book News from Leenie Brown
(bit.ly/LeenieBBookNews)
~*~*~
Turn the page to read an excerpt of another one
of Leenie's books

Persuading Miss Mary Excerpt

Would you like to know how Colonel Fitzwilliam's brother and Mary find happily ever after together? You can find out in *Persuading Miss Mary*.

Chapter 1

"What do you mean I am not allowed entrance?" Reginald Fitzwilliam, Viscount Westonbury, glared at Mr. Nibley, Matlock House's longtime butler.

"Just that, my lord. The countess has informed me that you are not allowed entrance without specific invitation."

"But it is my home!"

Mr. Nibley did not flinch. "Not at present, my lord. Your residence is the house in Brook Street."

"The house in Brook Street?" Wes huffed and looked at the sky above him before continuing. "I fully realize that my residence is in Brook Street. However, this is also my home, and I will not leave without seeing my mother."

Mr. Nibley paused for a moment as if considering whether or not he should disturb his mistress.

Wes waved toward the house. "My mother, if you will."

"I shall see if she is home to callers."

"I am not a caller! I am her son."

"Yes, my lord." Finally, the staid man before Wes shifted uneasily. "I only do as I am told, my lord."

Wes clenched his jaw and shook his head. "Am I allowed to wait inside while you check?"

Mr. Nibley gave a slight shake of his head. "I do apologize, my lord, but I have my orders."

"Oh, for the love of –," he stopped when Mr. Nibley coughed. "Yes, yes, I know. Mother cannot abide such language, and I promise to not resort to such as long as my mother sees me. If she will not, then I shall be forced to vent my spleen with whatever colourful language I choose and at whatever volume I wish to shout it."

The butler gave a nod of his head and hurried into Matlock House to see if his mistress was willing to see her eldest son, who was left to mutter oaths under his breath on the step and wonder what bee had flown into his mother's bonnet. She had not locked him out of the house in years!

The last time had been when a gentleman had shown up to collect a debt from Lord Matlock which had been incurred by his son, who should have been at school and not in some gambling hell. Being locked out of the house, coupled with the removal of his allowance until the sum had been repaid fully and half again, had worked well. Westonbury never set foot in a gambling hell after that, and his bills were always paid before word of any outstanding sums reached the ears of his mother.

For most gentlemen, their fathers were to be feared, and Lord Matlock was no exception. However, Lady Matlock was a good bit more fearsome to her sons than their father for she was cunning in her punishments, which were always doled out as if they were the most natural things in the world. If one took a step off a cliff, one must experience a fall. That was his mother's philosophy. Therefore, if you stole a biscuit, you spent the day in the kitchen assisting the scullery maid.

She loved her sons fiercely. Too fiercely at times, if you asked Lord Westonbury. He shook his head and chuckled. His mother had an uncanny ability to anticipate how he might attempt to escape a punishment or to find a bit of fun. She had been sitting below his window on more than one occasion at their estate when, as a young boy, he had been required to stay indoors for some indiscretion such as tormenting the stable cats.

The door opened interrupting Wes's contemplation of his mother.

"My lady will see you in the green sitting room, and only in the green sitting room."

Just as he suspected, she expected him to decide on where they would meet, which he had been considering. His mother was not fond of the small drawing room off of the library, and that would have been precisely where he would have told Nibley that his mother could meet him. But again, she had thwarted his enjoyment by anticipating his move.

He handed his hat and walking stick to Mr. Nibley before removing his great coat.

"Am I allowed to direct myself to said room, or must I wait to be announced?"

The right corner of Mr. Nibley's mouth tipped

upward but only just. "Do you wish to be announced, my lord?"

Wes chuckled. Mr. Nibley might appear to be wholly stoic, but he was not immune to the desire to have a bit of fun on occasion. "Indeed, I think I must be if I am merely a caller. Do you remember my name?"

"The name you use at every house, my lord?"

"No, the one that is precisely designed to annoy my mother."

"I think I do."

"Then, lead on my good man, and I shall not turn you out when I become master of Matlock House."

"I am sure I will not even be alive when that happens, my lord."

"I do hope that is not true. Not that I am wishing for my father's demise, of course."

"I did not think you were, my lord." Mr. Nibley began leading Wes down the hall to the green sitting room. The only sitting room on the ground floor — the room which was designated for calls and not much else.

The upper servant stepped into the room and, in a voice he might use if he were speaking to someone at the other end of a grand ballroom filled with dancers awaiting the start of the music, said "My lord, Reginald Arthur Fitzwilliam, Viscount Westonbury, the first-born and heir of the body of Lord Matlock, long may he live, to see Lady Matlock."

"Nibley," Lady Matlock scolded.

"I am only doing my duty, my lady," the butler replied with a bow before ducking out of the room.

"If he were not put up to such a thing by you, I would see him reprimanded properly."

"No, you would not," Wes said as he took a chair near where his mother was perched on her favourite sofa with a dog next to her. "Is that not Darcy's beast?"

"Beast? Dash is not a beast, are you, boy?" His mother scratched Dash's ear. "He is here to keep your brother company while he recovers."

"Then why is he here rather than with Richard?"

"Why are you here?"

Wes raised an eyebrow at his mother's coy response. "Because this is the only room in which I was allowed." He crossed his arms and leveled a disdainful look in Lady Matlock's direction. "Would you care to explain to me what I have done that has resulted in my exile from my home?"

"You are banned from the house in Brook Street?"

"Mother."

She chuckled and shrugged. "Impertinence is rather bothersome; is it not?"

"Yes, Mother. Now, if you would answer me seriously."

"I have guests."

"That is no reason for me to be stopped at the door to my home."

She shrugged again. "It is if the father of one of my guests has expressed concern regarding you."

Wes's brow furrowed. Who was visiting his mother?

"And, since the arrival of my guests, I have heard a most disturbing story from one of them."

"I still do not –"

"About you."

"I beg your pardon? You have heard a disturbing story about me?"

"Yes." She fluttered her lashes at him but said no more.

For a full minute, he only glared at her. It was a futile attempt to goad her into speaking, and he knew it. Still, it had to be attempted. "Oh, very well, what have I done?"

"I understand Miss Lydia and her sister met you in London." She lifted her chin slightly. "Quite often the ladies at such places as where you met them have been tossed out of their homes."

His waiting on the front step was beginning to make sense.

"Now, I know that there are gentlemen who frequent such places." She watched her hand stroke Dash's fur rather than looking at him. A faint pink tinged her cheeks. "However, they are not where I would wish my son to –"

"Please, Mother. I understand your meaning." He was likely as uncomfortable with this topic of conversation as she was. "However, I believe I am old enough to make my own decisions about such things."

She sighed. "Of course, you are." Her voice was just above a whisper and laced with disappointment. She lifted her eyes to him. "I only wished to make my point."

"I shall consider what you have said."

"Thank you."

"Am I reinstated as someone who can visit without an invitation?"

She shook her head. "I fear not. As long as Miss Lydia and Miss Bennet are staying here, you must be a stranger."

Wes blinked. "Miss Lydia and Miss Bennet are here?" Miss Mary Bennet was here at his parents' home? Walking the halls he had walked all his life? Sleeping in one of their guest rooms?

"Yes, I thought it good to have an ally in seeing that Richard recovers as he should, and, since Miss Kitty is visiting Georgiana, Miss Mary was sent to keep her sister company. However, there is not a lot of love lost between you and Miss Mary, so her father was concerned that being in a place where you might meet regularly might provoke her into besmirching the Bennet name. You know how it is. If someone should be calling and hear a young lady speaking plainly to a gentleman, the young lady will be the one taken to task."

"I would not provoke her."

His mother's replying look told him that she did not believe such a thing was possible, and truth be told, it likely was not. Miss Mary did not treat him as anyone else did – save for his closest family members and best friend. To her, he was merely a gentleman – not a viscount or the future Earl of Matlock. And confound it all if it was not refreshing!

"Then, am I only allowed to call during proper hours and in only this room, or will I be allowed to visit my brother?"

His mother sighed. "Your father will say you are welcome to visit your brother and join us for dinner and all those such things. However, neither he nor I will tolerate any provocation of our guests."

Wes nodded.

"I like her."

Wes's brow furrowed. "Miss Lydia?"

"Yes, her, but also her sister. Miss Mary is no wilting wallflower. I quite approve of that even if she does need a little softening."

Her head tilted to the side as she looked at him. So, this was her true purpose. She saw Miss Mary as a project of sorts.

"Just be kind to her," she added. "That is all I ask. Treat her as you would Georgiana."

That was a little bit impossible. He had never had a dream about Georgiana being in his bed. However, he was not about to say such to his mother. Instead, he dutifully assured her that he would do his best to behave as she expected.

"And if you could stop frequenting that place – Sally's, I believe it is called."

"Mother."

"I just think it would help you improve in the eyes of Miss Mary."

"I said I would consider what you had said. I will not promise any further."

She sighed. "I suppose I will have to be satisfied with that."

"Yes, you will. Now, am I allowed to see my brother?"

Lady Matlock glanced at the clock before rising. "Yes, I do believe he will be rising and making his way to the library."

"Rising? Do not tell me he is still taking a rest each afternoon." He rose to follow her from the room, but Dash stepped between Wes and his mother.

"He most certainly is. But it is not my doing." She smiled over her shoulder at him.

"Miss Lydia?"

She nodded. "As I said, I wanted to have an ally in seeing Richard recover."

Wes laughed as he followed his mother and Dash up the stairs. "Have I complimented you lately on your deviousness?"

"No, I do not believe you have," she replied with a chuckle. "There is a soiree that you must attend the day after next."

"Mother."

"You must marry someday, Reginald. The nursery has been empty for far too long."

"You forget, my lady," he said as he came to a stop on the landing next to her. "My residence is in Brook Street."

She patted his cheek. "Only until you marry. Then, you are free to bring my daughter and your children here to be with me."

Acknowledgements

There are many who have had a part in the creation of this story. Some have read and commented on it. Some have proofread for grammatical errors and plot holes. Others have not even read the story and a few, I know, will never read it. However, their encouragement and belief in my ability, as well as their patience when I became cranky or when supper was late or the groceries ran low, was invaluable.

And so, I would like to say *thank you* to Zoe, Rose, Kristine, Ben, and Kyle as well as my patrons on Patreon and the readers who faithfully read all those Thursday posts on my blog. I feel blessed by your help, support, and understanding.

I have not listed my dear husband in the above group because, to me, he deserves his own special thank you, for, without his somewhat pushy insistence that I start sharing my writing, none of my writing goals and dreams would have been met.

~*~*~

For those who might be interested in some of the visual inspiration I used while writing this book — I have a Pinterest board for that.

Other Leenie B Books

You can find all of Leenie's books at this link
bit.ly/LeenieBBooks
where you can explore the collections below

~*~

Other Pens, Mansfield Park

~*~

Touches of Austen Collection

~*~

Other Pens, Pride and Prejudice

~*~

Dash of Darcy and Companions Collection

~*~

Marrying Elizabeth Series

~*~

Willow Hall Romances

~*~

The Choices Series

~*~

Darcy Family Holidays

~*~

Darcy and... An Austen-Inspired Collection

About the Author

Leenie Brown has always been a girl with an active imagination, which, while growing up, was both an asset, providing many hours of fun as she played out stories, and a liability, when her older sister and aunt would tell her frightening tales. At one time, they had her convinced Dracula lived in the trunk at the end of the bed she slept in when visiting her grandparents!

Although it has been years since she cowered in her bed in her grandparents' basement, she still has an imagination which occasionally runs away with her, and she feeds it now as she did then — by reading!

Her heroes, when growing up, were authors, and the worlds they painted with words were (and still are) her favourite playgrounds! Now, as an adult, she spends much of her time in the Regency world, playing with the characters from her favourite Jane Austen novels and those of her own creation.

When she is not traipsing down a trail in an attempt to keep up with her imagination, Leenie resides in the beautiful province of Nova Scotia with her two sons and her very own Mr. Brown (a wonderful mix of all the best of Darcy, Bingley, and Edmund with a healthy dose of the teasing Mr. Tilney and just a dash of the scolding Mr. Knightley).

Connect with Leenie

E-mail:

LeenieBrownAuthor@gmail.com

Facebook:

www.facebook.com/LeenieBrownAuthor

Blog:

leeniebrown.com

Patreon:

https://www.patreon.com/LeenieBrown

Subscribe to Leenie's Mailing List:

Book News from Leenie Brown

(bit.ly/LeenieBBookNews)

www.ingramcontent.com/pod-product-compliance
Lightning Source LLC
Chambersburg PA
CBHW060857250626
47159CB00008B/2784